Evaluation and Credentialing in Digital Music Communities

W0193292

This report was made possible by grants from the John D. and Catherine T. MacArthur Foundation in connection with its grant making initiative on Digital Media and Learning. For more information on the initiative visit http://www.macfound.org.

The John D. and Catherine T. MacArthur Foundation Reports on Digital Media and Learning

A complete series list can be found at the back of the book.

Evaluation and Credentialing in Digital Music Communities

Benefits and Challenges for Learning and Assessment

H. Cecilia Suhr

The MIT Press
Cambridge, Massachusetts
London, England

MIT Press books may be purchased at special quantity discounts for business or sales promotional use. For information, please email special_sales@mitpress.mit.edu.

This book was set in Stone by the MIT Press. Printed and bound in the United States of America.

Library of Congress Cataloging-in-Publication Data

Suhr, H. Cecilia (Hiesun Cecilia), 1979–.
Evaluation and credentialing in digital music communities : benefits and challenges for learning and assessment / H. Cecilia Suhr.
    pages   cm.—(John D. and Catherine T. MacArthur Foundation reports on digital media and learning)
Includes bibliographical references and index.
ISBN 978-0-262-52714-9 (pbk. : alk. paper)
1. Indaba Music (Electronic resource). 2. Spotify. 3. Online social networks. 4. Music—Internet marketing. I. Title.
ML74.7.S84   2014
780.285′4678—dc23
2014017229

10   9   8   7   6   5   4   3   2   1

Contents

Series Foreword

The John D. and Catherine T. MacArthur Foundation Reports on Digital Media and Learning, published by the MIT Press, in collaboration with the Monterey Institute for Technology and Education (MITE), present findings from current research on how young people learn, play, socialize and participate in civic life. The Reports result from research projects funded by the MacArthur Foundation as part of its $50 million initiative in digital media and learning. They are published openly online (as well as in print) in order to support broad dissemination and to stimulate further research in the field.

1 Introduction

The evaluation of music has long been part of the cultural and media discourse, including reviews in newspapers, magazines, press coverage, ratings, the Billboard charts, and online commentaries. Often a key cultural intermediary, such as an artist and repertoire (A&R) agent, makes a decision based on a particular work's potential mass appeal (Zwaan, ter Bogt, and Raaijmakers 2009). Upon public release of an album, the press plays a significant role that can "make or break" musicians' careers (Brennan 2006).

While music critics play a vital role in evaluating and critiquing music, fans also evaluate music through online reviews, and the significance of fan reviews can go beyond simple expressions of likes and dislikes. For example, the progressive rock genre has been shaped by fan reviews and discourses through resolving competing definitions in hegemonic tension (Ahlkvist 2011).

With the rise of participatory fan culture (Jenkins 2006), aspiring and professional musicians alike have used social media as a vital platform for showcasing and promoting their music. As insightfully noted by Brown (2012):

The greatest change wrought by the advent of new media is in facilitating a groundswell of amateur and semi-professional musicians in the same way that the provision of public sporting facilities enables wider participation in amateur sport and an explosion of professional sports. (17)

In this respect, Keen (2008) has argued that the democratization of amateur cultural productions in digital environments has resulted in the degradation of cultural standards.[1] Yet the ubiquity of amateur cultural production in digital environments seems to have rapidly increased the evaluation practices in recent times. Rating, ranking, voting, "liking," and "friending" have all become the fabric of social media activities today, and ordinary users, peers, and critics subsequently play an integral role as cultural intermediaries.

In the early days of social media, marked by the birth of Myspace in 2003, the evaluation of music was reflected in the ongoing valorization of popularity (i.e., quantity and numbers). In a previous work, *Social Media and Music* (Suhr 2012), I offered a preliminary analysis of how musicians gain popularity on social networking sites and the subsequent conversion of popularity into social, economic, and cultural capital. In this study and others (Suhr 2009, 2010), I used applied social protocols, Hardt and Negri's (2000) frameworks of immaterial and affective labor, and Terranova's (2004) concept of free labor to analyze musicians' efforts to gain popularity on social networking sites. The goal of this analysis was to examine the emergence of voluntary activities in digital environments. Indeed, as a testament to how important these laboring practices are for gaining popularity, the number of books and services on how to increase popularity is on the rise. Inasmuch as the practice of social protocols, tips, and techniques may seem tangential and frivolous from the standpoint of the judgment and evaluation of music, in a close analysis, these activities are often intricately interwoven, yielding a synergistic impact.

Recently, evaluations have become more complex, no longer focusing solely on gaining popularity through adopting particular social protocols or spamming others relentlessly in social media platforms. The evaluations of music have become diversified through various contest mechanisms and have even been monetized through an array of website services. Slicethepie.com, songpeople.com, musicxray.com, and hitpredictor.com are examples of sites that promote useful feedback for musicians. On some of these sites, random audience members are paid to give feedback and critiques.

Another development in music evaluations is the process of credentialing through digital badges. Digital badges have recently emerged as a potential alternative credentialing method in informal learning environments. Digital Media and Learning and the MacArthur Foundation have funded preliminary exploratory studies of this method, which paralleled Mozilla's groundbreaking Open Badges program. Participating organizations that issue badges through Mozilla's Open Badges program are mainly in the fields of education, games, and informal learning organizations, although a few cultural organizations are also involved, such as the Dallas Museum of Art and the Smithsonian American Art Museum. Given the widespread and rapid increase of evaluation and credentialing in digital music communities, at the time of analysis, music was noticeably absent in Mozilla's Open Badges program. Yet this absence does not mean that badge issuing has not taken place in digital music communities. Although in a much more limited and discursive context, digital badges were offered on Microsoft's Zune Social site. In 2008, digital badges were awarded to site users who listened to artists or albums, as well as those who contributed to forums and music reviews. However, this social networking site did not gain much momentum, and in the end some controversy arose surrounding the community's failure (Newman 2011). Similar to Zune's practices, Spotify's playlists also issue badges for those who function as music curators and digital DJs. Although digital badges were developed to encourage fans and music listeners to participate as a new type of tastemakers, few digital music communities have adopted digital badges to aid in assessment and evaluation. In this context, this study explores digital music communities' use of digital badges as a reward for both casual music evaluators and musicians. The first case study focuses on audience evaluation via playing Spotify's Hit or Not game, where game players evaluate a song's hit potential and receive digital badges as rewards. In this vein, the first case study explores the gamification of learning and evaluation; when the act of music evaluation turns into a game, what do the players learn, and what may be the implications of this type of evaluation? The second, more in-depth case study on Indaba Music examines the process of gaining badges through involvement in contests. In addition, I explore whether or not gaining badges holds significance for musicians. Taken as a whole, this report analyzes how digital badges are perceived by both music listeners and musicians. To what extent can digital badges offer an effective way to represent and credit musicians' accomplishments and merits? What are the emerging challenges, benefits, and shortcomings in the use of digital badges as an alternative evaluation mechanism? How do the uses of digital badges in the context of assessing creativity intersect or diverge with the practices related to education and other noncreative fields?

Overall this report contends that using digital badges as a means of assessment or credentialing in digital music communities poses a unique set of challenges and shortcomings. A comparison with the educational context makes this clear. Although several researchers are concerned about the gamification of education (Domínguez et al. 2013; Lee and Hammer 2011), in digital music communities such as Indaba Music, the process of acquiring a badge involves more complex assessment processes, such as peer, amateur, and expert evaluations. Many musicians' efforts at reputation building and portfolio creation serve as important links with the music industry's acceptance and recognition. However, unlike the notion of symbolic capital (Bourdieu 1984), whereby honor and prestige are acquired through collective understanding, digital badges have thus far not gained collective value among Spotify game players and Indaba musicians. Much of this is due to the mainstream music industry's assessment criteria. The unique culture emerging in the digital spaces also plays a part, though, as the criteria, assessments, and meaning-making processes are often intricately interwoven and sometimes in conflict with the music industry's ideologies and norms. Yet it is also important to realize that when it comes to understanding the evolution of a certain dominant criterion, one should consider Negus's (1998) point that music production "does not take place simply 'within' a corporate environment created according to the requirements of capitalist production but in relation to broader culture formations and practices" (360). The newly emerging norms, criteria, and standards in digital environments are also shaped by the culture in which they thrive.

In understanding the emerging evaluation methods, tools, and credentialing systems, one must account for multiple aspects, including human agency, resistance, emerging norms, social protocols, and individual motivations, as well as the ideological undercurrents and the culture of the particular institutions that grant the credentials and merits. Thus an analysis of emerging evaluation practices in the digital environment is ideally situated at the nexus of social, technological, and complex hegemonic cultural practices.

Theoretical Overview

The underlying premise for this research draws on several interconnected themes. Although the context of the research stems from the intersection between digital media studies and popular music studies, the relevant modes of inquiry are not exclusive to one particular discipline. A concentration on a certain discipline's prominent interests would limit the scope of this study to a reductionist inquiry, inevitably reducing the research conclusions to a binary format. A typical question potentially asked in a micro-context would be: Are badges effective measuring tools for the evaluation of music? In a macro-perspective, the attention would focus on digital capitalism and the economy and would seek to answer such questions as: Are digital communities of music empowering or exploitative places? My goal is to avoid posing questions that require deterministic answers. Instead I am convinced that the question about evaluation is neither a debate about the good-or-bad dichotomization nor an issue solely limited to the educational context. Rather, the significant issues traverse an array of disciplines, such as game studies, education, popular music studies, critical cultural studies, advertising and marketing, philosophy, sociology, computer-mediated communication, social psychology, and ethnomusicology. To this end, my goal is to unpack the topic of evaluation from various overlapping perspectives.

At this juncture, a brief overview of some of the pressing issues within the context of the popular music industry is imperative. Various long-standing issues, such as the dichotomy between commerce and art, extend through today, and we cannot jump into a discussion on evaluation without locating the ideological stance and position of the evaluative platforms. Many scholars have sought to understand the tensions between art and commerce, and between high art and popular music (Gracyk 2007; Negus 1995). In a capitalist society, musicians' quests to be creative and artistic are often considered at odds with the profit-driven music industry (Stratton 1982, 1983). Negus (1999) explores the intersection between culture, industry, and musical creativity and argues that "culture produces an industry," thereby rejecting the view that the music industry is only "governed by an organizational logic or structure" (14). In line with this view, Frith (1996) notes that the art/commerce boundary is flawed and reductionist, contending that both A&R (artist and repertoire) agents (those who recruit rising talents) and artists view art and commerce in tandem, rather than as disparate issues (90).

Another dichotomy analogous to the art/commerce tension is the tension between mainstream record labels and independent labels. Over time, the distinction between these two types of labels has gradually decreased (Hesmondhalgh 1999; Strachan 2007). Yet one aspect that cannot be ignored is that, in comparison to the smaller labels, the bigger the firm, the stronger the focus will be on profit maximization (Wikstrom 2010). Similarly, independent musicians continue to voice their concerns about compromised creativity (Brown 2012). Nonetheless the sound and direction of musical creativity are determined not only at the level of production but also through distribution channels, which function as another level of gatekeeping. Radio has always been a staple of the music industry's critical distribution channels in terms of promotions, often achieved through a payola practice, which involves paying radio station DJs to play select songs on air (Segrave 1994). College radio stations, on the other hand, are often known as supportive and viable alternative platforms for indie music. Yet there has been a struggle to maintain this independence; Desztich and McClung (2007) and Waits (2008) note that the music industry has also gradually permeated college radio stations in regard to what music gets selected for airplay.

Although the corporate music industry still holds power, scholarly discourses on musicians' do-it-yourself (DIY) practices have also increased. In the past, DIY culture was constructed in the context of punk music, a genre in which resistance to commercialized music was a central ethos and part of punk's musical identity (Dunn 2012; Lee 1995). DIY practices have also been discussed in live music and social media (Lingel and Naaman 2011), have been explored in relation to the unique ideological formations shaping its creative identity (Mōri 2009), and have been lauded for their democratic potential in helping Internet labels to create alternative niche music outlets without posing a threat to major record labels (Galuszka 2012). However, musicians can rarely remain completely autonomous from the music industry or from corporate culture. Dale (2009) also rightly points out that Internet-based social networks may still generate questions about power structures among DIY musicians: "For those interested in producing the kind of counter-hegemonic agency ... questions of power and power relations remain pressing" (191). Without a doubt, the reconfiguration of dominant and subordinate forces deserves critical attention, and I argue that despite alternative modes of sharing and distribution, dominant power is maintained by the music industry. This is evident when we consider how social media environments have turned into a testing ground for many emerging artists, some of whom have been scouted by major record labels after attaining social capital (Suhr 2012). Often the discourse surrounding musicians' success stories emphasizes getting noticed by someone affiliated with the music industry or gaining the mainstream industry's recognition. These success stories are frequently featured on Indaba Music and other sites as testimony to the optimistic view that "you, too, can be the next one." It is important to also note how musicians perceive the DIY trend, and whether or not this development is considered an impediment to their career management and advancement.

In this report, I reveal that DIY musicians do not maintain their DIY status exclusively or strictly apart from the potential to stop having to "do it themselves." According to these research data, musicians often compete in contests and competitions because of their ties to the music industry; rather than completely resisting the music industry's role or justifying its presence, musicians view the competitions as a means to gain potential professional "work made for hire" opportunities. However, work-for-hire opportunities provided on Indaba Music have varying rules, depending on each contest. For instance, in one of the contests, a remix contest for ZZ Ward's song "365 Days," the rules indicate the following conditions:

In the event that an Entrant's Remix cannot be deemed a "work made for hire," the Entrant agrees to assign away and transfer any and all rights in their Remix to Hollywood Records, Inc., or a designee of Hollywood Records, Inc. Entrants shall have no ownership rights or interest whatsoever in the applicable Remix and the underlying musical composition(s) embodied therein, and shall not commercially use or exploit the Remix in any manner whatsoever. (Indaba Music.com)

In another contest, Et Musique Pour Tous, the "entrant shall own the copyright to their submission" (Indaba Music.com).

Seiter and Seiter (2012) note that in the legal domain, copyrights are often relinquished in the cases in which the clients for work-for-hire situations are creative producers. On Indaba Music, although there are contests wherein the musicians still hold copyrights, other contests that require the entrants to give up copyrights may be exploitative. However, even if no financial gain may be achieved, musicians often get involved for the chance to be discovered through their exposure, which serves as an immaterial exchange value for musicians (Suhr 2012).

The topic of copyright and artists' compensation in the digital era is an increasingly alarming issue and undoubtedly requires serious scrutiny. Given the limited scope of this report, I focus on the ambiguous and blurred lines between work and play, analogous to "interest-driven" activities: "Interest-driven genres of participation characterize engagement with specialized activities, interests, or niche and marginalized identities. In contrast to friend-driven participation, kids establish relationships that center on their interests, hobbies, and career aspirations rather than friendship per se" (Ito et al. 2009, xvii). Although this definition is based on youth participation in digital environments, the essence of these activities extends to all musicians, regardless of age. The stakes for musicians, however, are high, as the winners of competitions often receive rewards, the most important being potential connections to the music industry. To this extent, the music industry's involvement in digital environments can be an undeniably attractive and propelling drive for many musicians seeking connections. One way to understand this phenomenon is to view musicians as "cultural entrepreneurs," echoing Scott's (2012) observation:

What motivates these homologous cultural entrepreneurs to engage in productive activities for minimal or limited financial return is either the promise of exposure or the opportunity to engage in activities that are in line with their career aspirations and identities. These favours are intrinsically interesting and rewarding at an artistic level—affording the opportunity to help fellow artists, which may initiate what may be a fruitful and enduring relationship. (238–239)

Another prominent trend tied to cultural entrepreneurship is the evaluation and judgment of music by the hybrid array of traditional and emerging cultural intermediaries. Some evaluations are traditional because they are established and controlled by the music industry's long-established way of selecting and discerning potential talent. Other intermediaries are new on the scene and are operating in tandem with the advancement of technology through algorithms and social networks (e.g., peer comments, listening records, and votes). These frameworks are not unique, but what is innovative is how they are now operating together as one comprehensive mechanism.

Three Views of Music Evaluations

Music evaluations can loosely be categorized into three views. The first is based on an ethical dimension, broadly discussed under aesthetics as ethics, or *ethestics*, by various scholars in the philosophy of art (N. Carroll 2000; Gaut 1998). Carroll (2000) states that much of this view of aesthetics as ethics was not accepted or embraced in the past. As autonomism argues, "Artworks … are valuable for their own sake, not because of their service to ulterior purposes, such as moral enlightenment or improvement" (351). However, in defense of the negative charges made against an ethical framing of aesthetics, Gaut (1998) notes that "ethicism does not entail the casual thesis that good art ethically improves people" (183). Despite the controversial outlook on art's value stemming from ethics, the influential writings of Adorno and the Frankfurt theorists on the value of the arts embed this outlook in capitalism. In their seminal essay, Adorno and Horkheimer (2002) hierarchized art's value based on the dichotomy between high and low art. They further argued that only autonomous art, devoid of capitalistic features, could empower individual and social progress. In particular, Adorno has been divisive because of his understanding of the notion of popular music, which creates a dichotomy between "serious music" and "nonserious music" (Adorno 1998). For Adorno, formulaic, repetitive, and profit-driven popular music does not further the critical analysis of music but only promotes passive and regressive listening behavior (Adorno 1978).

An ethical approach to understanding music and aesthetic tastes intersects with the second perspective related to the evaluation of music, which is based on listeners' relationships to music. In short, the question arises here: What does the music listener experience? Is it qualitatively good or bad? Langer (1966) notes the interconnection between feelings and aesthetic experience when she states that "the arts objectify subjective reality, and subjectify outward experience of nature. Art education is the education of feeling, and a society that neglects it gives itself up to formless emotion. Bad art is corruption of feeling" (12). For Langer, the aesthetic experience one feels can be categorized into the good/ bad dichotomy; good art is supposed to yield good feelings, and bad art logically produces bad feelings. Therefore the ethical factor is related to the feelings connected with the aesthetic experience. However, for Levinson (1996), the presence of pleasure or displeasure cannot be a qualified measure of art's value:

Many artworks unmistakably offer us rewards that do not naturally cash out as pleasure or enjoyment at any level, rewards that are at least distinct from and independent of any pleasure or enjoyment that may attach to them. (12)

Echoing the notion of Kant's (1952) "disinterestedness," where pleasure is linked with sensuality and lower forms of aesthetic experiences, is good music supposed to create displeasure? Shumway (2008) asserts that values and pleasures are linked to the judgment of arts and aesthetic quality. However, he further distinguishes between two types of pleasures: "The way in which the idea of the aesthetic is most often used is to maintain that pleasure in beauty is fundamentally different from the pleasures of the senses, or the 'lower pleasures'" (107).

Reflecting earlier discussions on the symbiotic relationship between music and feelings, Frith (1996) also notes how the assessment and evaluation of music inevitably intersect with one's personal feelings about the music.

What's really at issue is feeling. In the end "bad music" describes an emotional rather than an ideological judgment. We don't like a record; we then seek to account for that dislike. ... Feelings, particularly feelings of like or dislike—for music, for people—are often surprising, contradictory, and disruptive, they go against what we're supposed to feel, what we'd like to feel. (72–73)

This outlook produces a significant binary that we must wrestle with in the context of music listening. If music somehow provides us a pleasurable experience, then music must be, by nature, good. However, we still have an unsettling question to answer: Whose experience matters? Is it the experience of an "authority" or of the masses? This leads us to the third evaluation method, based on the dichotomy between quantity versus quality.

The highest recognition in music evaluations in capitalistic societies has often been considered the concept of "hit" music. In this view, quantity speaks volumes about a specific song's or work's quality. Within this framework, the more people consume a song, the better its value is deemed to be; therefore the goal for any song should be to be liked by many individuals. Adorno, as one of the most outspoken scholars to critique hit music, defines a hit as commodified music that results from industrial mass production that seeks to increase profit margins. Hit music is most incisively critiqued for its standardization (Adorno 1998), as music becomes imitative of other works that were previously proved to be successful. However, despite the argument that the masses may desire familiarity in music, "standardization in radio produces its veil of pseudo-individuality" (Adorno 1945, 216). In other words, repetition and familiarity do not exist overtly but are masked by the pretense of originality and uniqueness, thereby creating an illusion that consumers have a choice: "The less the listener has to choose, the more is he made to believe that he has a choice" (216).

Considering the music industry's interest in profitability, the hit song has been a central aspect across all genres, including country music (Jaret 1982). Hit music in the commercial music industry is clearly recognized through the ranking system of the charts. To this end, the music charts are considered "useful decision support tools that influence the visibility and success of artists, as well as help calculate their financial rewards" (Bhagwan, Grandison, and Gruhl 2009). As Parker (1991) also notes, "In theory, the charts define the most popular of popular music, the goal, the pinnacle of success" (205). While the Billboard chart epitomizes commercial success, the metric is not without controversy. In the week of January 20, 1990, *Billboard* magazine introduced a new system of technology that measured a detailed profile of listeners (Breen 1990). As Breen sharply pointed out, this so-called scientific system only "represents the refinement of the commodification of popular music" (370).

Research Methods

The primary research method that I used in this study was a qualitative method including interviews, surveys, and textual analysis of Spotify and Indaba Music. I chose this methodological approach in support of Belk's assertion that "mixed methods are often seen as eclectic, pluralistic, and rejecting traditional dualism" (Belk 2007, 199).

Although Spotify's main function is to provide convenient access to countless music files readily available for streaming, Spotify also developed many diverse applications (apps) to engage music listeners in eclectic ways. This report specifically explores Spotify's game app Hit or Not as a case study. I gathered the data via textual analysis, involvement as a participant-observer, and sample interviews with other game players of Hit or Not. The seventeen game players ranged in age from eighteen to fifty-three, and they were recruited in a variety of ways: invitations on Facebook, visits to Spotify's Hit or Not fan page on Facebook (which no longer exists), and the use of a research assistant's personal network. The phone interview data collection period lasted approximately eight to nine months. Besides interviews, this research also includes a textual analysis of the Hit or Not game and other data pertaining to the game designs and rules and rewards displayed on the Spotify app.

Indaba Music, on the other hand, is a cloud-based collaboration platform where many contests are held for aspiring and professional musicians. Musicians earn many different types of badges, but most prominently through their contest results. For this study, I explored Indaba Music's evaluation process and analyzed musicians' perceptions of digital badges as conveyors of honors and prestige. The research was extensive in its scope, drawing on data from the responses of 255 international participants via a survey created on SurveyMonkey. To generate a diverse participant pool, my research assistant and I reviewed the recent contest submissions and contacted the competitors directly via e-mail with the survey link. The survey used both open-ended questions and multiple-choice questions. The survey ran from July 2012 to February 2013, and the findings resulted in more than 130 pages of survey data, supplemented by data drawn from phone interviews with the five finalists of the Grammy U: The Masters' Critique contest, by a textual analysis of the entire Indaba Music site (including the large comments sections and discussion forums), and by interviews with the site's cofounder and the vice president of content management. In addition, this study includes in-depth, face-to-face interviews with twelve New York City–based musicians who are members of Indaba Music and have also each competed in Indaba Music contests at least once. The interviews took place between July 2012 and April 2013. Each interview lasted between twenty and sixty minutes, resulting in lengthy and informative transcripts. Due to the condensed format of this study, it is important to note that this report focuses only on select research findings; the in-depth implications of Indaba Music will need to be elaborated in another publication.

Chapter Overview

Following this introduction, chapter 2 explores how consumers pursue evaluations in digital environments, focusing on Spotify's Hit or Not game. In this chapter, I explore the intersection of evaluation and gamification, seeking to answer the question: How does gamification affect the evaluations, especially regarding motivations and rewards? I present an exploratory study of digital evaluations through interviews with game players, as well as a detailed analysis of the game's premises, rules, and rewards. As a whole, the chapter aims to chart and map the gamification of the evaluation territory.

Chapter 3 concentrates on the development of peer and professional critics on Indaba Music. Musicians earn badges mainly through winning contests or becoming finalists, runners-up, or honorable mentions in contests. This chapter illustrates how earning a badge is not just considered part of the gaming experience. In this vein, I challenge the notion that badges are a simple reward system, and instead focus on a detailed account of contest procedures, rewards, and judgments within the Indaba Music environment. A case study of the Grammy U contest was conducted to understand the winner's and the finalists' experiences. I also explore informal learning and in-person critiques from the music industry professionals. In general, the chapter evaluates the emerging challenges and shortcomings of contest-based virtual communities.

Chapter 4 examines the potential for badges to represent a symbol of honor. I explore the evolution of badges on Indaba Music and explain how badges are perceived by Indaba musicians. As part of the analysis, I further investigate musicians' motivational levels (intrinsic/extrinsic) and explore the challenges and shortcomings of badges as related to the issue of access in learning and credentialing institutions.

The final chapter summarizes the outcomes of this study and theorizes the working definition of digital evaluations. In doing so, this chapter argues for the need to study the digital evaluation phenomenon across the broad array of creative productions as they exist in digital environments.

2 Evaluation of Music by Audience: Spotify's "Hit or Not" Game

Deciding what music to listen to is a significant part of deciding and announcing to people not just who you "want to be," as a Prudential commercial has it, but who you are.

—Nicholas Cook, *Music: A Very Short Introduction*

Introduction

The practice of earning badges in game-centered websites has been on the rise. As Hamari and Eranti (2011) observe, the phenomenon of badges and trophies as a reward system in gaming environments has received little scholarly attention; similarly, academic research on the gamification of music evaluation hardly exists. To help remedy this shortcoming, this chapter conducts an exploratory study of one emerging music evaluation app, Spotify's Hit or Not game. Spotify is a digital music site where users can access millions of songs instantly. The site was founded in Sweden in October 2008 by Daniel Ek. To date, the service reportedly has more than 24 million users in twenty-eight different countries (Spotify). One noteworthy aspect of Spotify's service is its motto, Music Is Social. As an extension of this motto, Spotify has created a variety of applications to stimulate the interests of music listeners. This chapter strives to analyze the implications of gamifying music evaluation by exploring (1) how game players' motivation to gain points and badges affect their music evaluation process, and consequently, (2) how such motivations or the lack thereof relate to the shaping collective music standards. In addition, this study addresses to what extent learning about others' tastes in music affect their personal preferences. In line with this focus, this chapter also overviews the specific context in which Spotify's streaming service dovetails with the shift that has taken place in audience consumption.

Reconceptualizing the Role of Audiences in the Digital Age

According to Frith (1996), at the beginning of the nineteenth century, good music was produced for its own sake and thus was autonomous from audience response. Subsequently critics were necessary to play the role of experts, "who can explain the music to the public, teach it how to listen" (64). Thus the gap between musicians and listeners widened, and critics valorized new and original music (Frith 1996, 65). With the emergence of commodity culture, Frith notes that this dynamic shifted a little; while mediation was still critical, the mass audiences' responses and reactions were more valued. In the digital era, the relationship between musicians and audiences has continued to hold tremendous value, although the new challenge is to track their preferences to help overcome audience fragmentation (Wikstrom 2010). Tied to this trend, the emergence of audience evaluation has become an integral part of digital environments.

An understanding of this new music industry model in the digital economy is critical in this context. Anderson (2014) notes that in the first decade of the twenty-first century, the extensive practice of piracy has transitioned to the legal downloading business. Tschmuck (2012) explains that before the launch of the iTunes music store in 2003, online services struggled owing to a lack of investment and licensed repertoire (191). However, soon after the birth of iTunes, other online retail stores emerged, such as Amazon.com in 2007 and Google Music in 2011. During this time, music streaming services were also on the rise and in direct competition with downloading services (Tschmuck 2012). According to Anderson (2014), while physical and digital sales have a common priority of making profit, the key difference is that digital services rely on "recommendation engines and social network engines" as their main driving force (64). To this end, the music industry—Spotify, Pandora, and iTunes—views audiences as the end users: "an actor that is essential to the formation, operation and sustenance of digital formations networks" (15). Anderson explains that "as third-party brokers, these networks that purchase and digest the information captured by these tools and services are key to structuring a significant portion of the new music industry" (28). This reconceptualization of audiences is important to consider, as it allows Spotify's game to be located within this specific cultural and economic climate.

Hit or Not

Given previous discussions, the primary way to understand the Hit or Not game (whose playlist is limited to the Warner Music Group music catalog) is to consider it as a new type of market research 2.0, encouraging interactivity and playful activity for participants while also serving as a new way to understand and predict consumers' likes, dislikes, and potential taste shifts. Upon opening Spotify's game app, players are given a consent box for agreement. The consent box states that the app "relies on the awesomeness of your collected votes to run smoothly." It clearly states the objectives of the game: "(1) making your voice heard regarding what music is hot and what is not; (2) getting points for your votes and receiving awesome badges; (3) competing with your friends" (Spotify, Hit or Not). Users have to consent to the following terms:

I understand that when I log into my Hit or Not account below, Hit or Not will be able to associate information about my Spotify use, such as library and listening history, with my Hit or Not account. Hit or Not's collection and use of this information will be governed by the WMG Privacy Policy. (Spotify, Hit or Not)

This statement sums up an obvious function of the game, namely, to serve as a digital surveillance tool to monitor users' preferences.

Hit or Not divides its songs into three broad genres: Party, Rock, and Urban. There is also an "All" category that lumps together these three genres. Audience evaluators can choose to play the game in a specific category, but the default setting is the "All" category. Negus (1999), in noting the importance of genres in the music industry, asserts that the demarcation of musical genres goes far beyond the mere categories of rap, pop, jazz, soul, rock, and so on. Rather, the genre concept serves as a way to cater to fans: "Fans are central to the production, reproduction, and circulation of numerous genres of music" (Negus 1999, 127). With the rise of online retailers and streaming services, Anderson notes that genres still serve as a viable tool to reach out to audiences, but notes that "the difference for iTunes and other digital services such as Amazon and Google that have established digital music retailers is that as they funnel their goods through genre categories the service accumulates data on their users" (70).

Besides probing the motives of the game from the online streaming service's point of view, we should ask how the game is understood by the game players themselves. Do they gain anything by playing the game, apart from the seemingly obvious reasons of sheer entertainment and playful activity? By motivating users to gain "badges" and allowing users to compete with one another, the game relies on the competitive aspect to disseminate musical preferences. To some extent, the game tests whether or not the game player has the ability to discern the "hit" factor. This aspect about the game caused much confusion among the game players. Participant 7 specifically expressed his frustration:

It's confusing. ... At first I thought ... "Hey I should learn a little bit more about what kind of music that people really like in this market or among the Spotify users." Then the second time that I played this game or the third time that I played this game, it's so weird that all the songs were not "Hits." You know it's not on the "Hit List." All of them? All of them. I played about 15–20 minutes all of them, maybe one or two it was on the "Hit List." I thought it was among people who played the same time. I do not know. To me at this point, if I play a little bit more or I spend more time with it and understand how the game is constructed a little bit better then I would be able to say anything. At this point, I think I'm a little confused.

Regardless of the game's actual intent, all the participants I talked to played according to their own personal musical preferences, not according to the explicit rules of the game. Participant 1 mentioned that he played the game based on his "own reaction to the music, whether or not it's a hit." Other participants also confirmed this view. Participant 1 expressed his confusion about the game and said he was "disappointed in the app." A similar reply was given by Participant 6, who thought that the possible underlying motive of the game was simply market research disguised as a playful, fun game:

I really resented that what they were doing was market research and they were trying to disguise it as something that I would think is fun. I was offended by their whole attitude in this "game" that really wasn't fun. They were just trying to get information out of me. A lot of times when I would listen I was trying to think of ways to sabotage their information. I was thinking, okay, if I say I like this group that I'm not supposed to like because of my previous answers, or my demographic. That will screw up their information.

Participant 2 further expressed his personal view that the game was "a cynical corporate tool."

I was offended when it was set up like you got more points if you guessed what everyone else guessed. If you went along with the crowd, you went along with popular opinion, then you were good and you were awarded. If you had your own opinion, you were alone in it. They were like, "Oh, sorry. You didn't agree with everybody else."

Similarly, Participant 8 expressed confusion: "I don't know why I'm being rewarded for guessing what everyone else likes, getting more points. I always guess what I like."

Although several participants related the game's purpose to market research and advertising, Participant 3 believed that the game "keeps one toward people's musical preferences." While all the participants who had played the game concurred that they did so according to their own penchants, one could potentially wonder if the game can affect the players' tastes as they learn about mass tastes, especially in light of gamification.

Gamifying Music Evaluation

According to Kapp (2012), gamification is not just about gaining points and badges:

Those things are elements of most games, and among the easier to implement, but those things alone do not [make] a game. The more challenging and beneficial aspects to gamification include the story, the challenge, the sense of control, decision making and a sense of mastery—these are the elements of games that are of the most value. (xviii)

While Hit or Not can be challenging and confusing to the users, one of the aspects that deserves to be explored is how gamification intersects with evaluation. Research on the intersection between gamification and learning has already been conducted by a variety of scholars (Muntean 2011; Raymer and Design 2011; Domínguez et al. 2013).

At this juncture, it is useful to ask how gamification affects the process of evaluation. The game players receive points and badges along the way. Each time a player guesses a song's hit viability, he or she earns points based on the percentage of players who have labeled a song a "hit" versus "not a hit." If one's assessment of a hit aligns with the majority of other players, one receives more points.

Badges are awarded throughout the game: First Point, On Your Way, Fresh Bread, Hipster Glasses, Tastemaker, One Hit Wonder, Pacemaker, Hit Predictor, On Fire, and so on. The use of badges as a way to reward game players is not new, and recent research has explored the intrinsic and extrinsic motivations related to the awarding of badges (Abramovich, Schunn, and Higashi 2013). Specifically, McDaniel, Lindgren, and Friskics (2012) explore the process of using a badging strategy in a gamified course at a visual arts and design school (University of Central Florida). The authors highlight different types of behavior associated with students' motivations to acquire badges and to engage in learning activities. Overall, the authors note that seeing peer achievements was an important motivator. Contrary to the previous research findings on badges and gamification in the context of education, evaluation games such as Hit or Not actually confront different issues.

For instance, if predicting the hit factor is rewarded, how does this relate to the manner in which evaluations are conducted? How do the badges motivate the players in this game? If acquiring badges is an important goal, do the badges motivate the players to align their tastes with hit music? Furthermore, how can the evaluation of musical tastes be considered right or wrong in the context of Hit or Not? To address this question, I asked the game players about their motivational level during the game. According to my interviewees, the badges did not motivate them to win or perform well while playing the game. In fact, many of them found the badges to be meaningless.

You know, as somebody who has played a lot of video games, it's nice, it's almost like a reward, but at the same time, they are kind of useless. That's like a, "Cool, I got that, but then that's it." It's like one second of feeling good but then after that it's irrelevant. Some of the crazier ones, like if it's a very specific badge, that carries a little bit more meaning because then you can go to your friend and say, "Ah, I got this badge." But other than that, no, they don't really do that much. (Participant 5)

Participant 5 further noted that the reason there is a lack of motivation or desire for acquiring badges was that the site users could not see or anticipate the types of badges available before playing.

I guess there's no motivation to earn a badge; the badge just comes, and it's like, "Cool, I got a badge for it." There's never any, because you don't really get to see what the badges are that you are trying to earn. In some other games, you do; you can see what badges you want to try to earn, and sometimes they are pretty incredible challenges that you try at—you do have motivation to tackle those challenges just because of how insane they are. But most of the time it's just kind of like—it just presents it to you after the fact, and you don't really notice that they've earned it or are trying to accomplish those badges. It's just like, "Oh, you did it, and now you get a badge." (Participant 5)

Another motivational factor in the game is competition. The game allows players to compare their points with their Facebook friends who have also played. The players are ranked in order, with the top ranked having the most points.

However, this aspect of the game did not seem to inspire the players to be more competitive. Both participants 6 and 7 replied that although they are very competitive individuals, in this particular game, earning points did not matter a great deal to them. Participant 6 added that he played "to find music, new music [he] likes, or maybe oldies music that [he has] forgotten about. In this case, the score isn't so important." Participant 9, however, noted that he was competitive about the game, but he remained adamant that playing it did not change or affect his personal tastes in music. Participant 17 claimed, "I just want to see what other opinions actually end up being as opposed to mine." Participant 2 also maintained the pointlessness of winning the game and further stated that he did not make any effort to win. Participant 4, however, claimed that although at first she was not motivated to score points and earn badges, as she "got into the game, [she] became more motivated to do that." As can be seen, these players' evaluation processes were not necessarily motivated by their desire to win but were mainly linked to their discernment of their own tastes and judgments related to music. Most of the players were distracted by how their musical taste aligned with the tastes of other players, and they focused little on which songs were potential hits. To this extent, encouraging the players to align their tastes with hit music did not influence the players. Yet what primarily affected their evaluation process was the negotiation between their own tastes and those of the others who played the game.

My Musical Tastes versus Others' Preferences

Given that the underlying premise of the game centered on a comparison of the players' taste preferences, it is important to further expound on how players in general view their own musical taste formation. The fields of social psychology and sociology have analyzed how personal preferences are shaped through close social networks and how they function as representations of self-identity.

Frith (1996) notes that "music constructs our sense of identity through the experiences it offers of the body, time, and sociability, experiences which enable us to place ourselves in imaginative cultural narratives" (275). Other scholars have also explored how personality and musical preferences relate to one another (Chamorro-Premuzic and Furnham 2007; Payne 1967; Hargreaves, Miell, and MacDonald 2002). Although this chapter does not cover the entire literature on this issue, several important research outcomes are pertinent to this study. In particular, Rentfrow and Gosling (2006) argue that there is a clear intersection between recognized groups of people in relation to their musical preferences. In a similar vein of research, young people clearly express their identities through the use of music (Rentfrow, McDonald, and Oldmeadow 2009). "Individuals prefer styles of music that reinforce and reflect aspects of their identities and personalities" (Rentfrow et al. 2009). Nonetheless shared musical tastes may not always yield positive outcomes, since these tastes can be a factor in misjudging (or stereotyping) others, especially among young people (Finnas 1987).

Most notably the discipline of sociology, Bourdieu's research on social class and cultural tastes comes to the fore. In dismissing Kantian aesthetics and their basis in the domain of "disinterestedness," Bourdieu (1984) argues that, rather than being universal in nature, cultural tastes are socially constructed and reflected through class hierarchy. He further discusses three different types of cultural tastes: the highbrow culture of the dominant class; the middlebrow taste, which reflects the middle class or petite bourgeoisie; and finally popular taste, which characterizes the lower classes. For Bourdieu, these distinctions are a critical way in which members of different classes distinguish themselves from other social groups by disassociating or opposing those tastes. However, understanding tastes is more complex than factors that only consider external backgrounds, that is, socioeconomic status or education levels. Holbrook and Schindler (1989) and Russell (1997) in particular observe how a variety of social influences, such as media, education, and family and peer networks, impact the formation of musical tastes; to this extent, he argues that musical tastes do not develop in an isolated context.

To make the matter even more complex, the individual's psychological or social background as related to taste is only one of the many approaches within the social sciences for studying musical and aesthetic tastes. Increasingly, many social media platforms allow individuals to publicly share information, photos, and other digital contents; these environments have created an emerging digital media culture where people are filling a new type of curatorial role (Hogan 2010).

A more specific example of this new digital behavior is the functioning of social media profiles as taste performances (Liu 2008). Given the diverse perspectives linked to musical tastes in relation to self-identity and external influences, it is worthwhile to further expound on how learning about other people's popular music preferences in digital environments has changed or affected the individual evaluation process. Upon posing these lines of inquiry, the majority of the survey participants gave definitive, short replies that others' opinions did not change their tastes in music even when they learned that others' tastes differed from theirs. A few participants elaborated on their responses:

"I mean, I like to listen to popular music at times just to get, just be updated, I guess, just to kind of understand what is popular, but it doesn't affect my taste at all, no" (Participant 5). "I often don't like the mainstream kind of music, so I have always been outside in that way" (Participant 6). In short, their answers seem to distance "popular music" as something not innately enjoyed but rather as "the other." Although class is not one of the factors explored in this study, many participants prefer to think of themselves as apart from, and more selective than, an imagined less-sophisticated "pop music" listener.

Learning about One's Musical Tastes: Reflexivity

According to Papastergiou (2009), "Games constitute potentially powerful learning environments" (1). To this extent, what do game players learn? The game players I interviewed noted that many of their tastes in music surprised them in comparison to others. Although participants did not view the game in terms of a traditional learning experience, much of the learning that took place in the game was informal as it relates to what Hennion (2007) calls reflexive activity. Listening is essentially a self-reflexive activity that allows listeners to learn about their own tastes in music. Hennion explains that music lovers are often apologetic and ashamed of their musical tastes, or they "accuse themselves of a practice that is too elitist, over-admit the ritual nature of their rock outings or love for opera" (5). Overall, in observing discourses about individual musical tastes, he notes how people are "so sociologized" (5). This view is interesting in light of how the players of Hit or Not discussed their musical tastes in relation to others. In this reflexive activity, listeners often position their views as either mainstream or nonmainstream, reflecting a socially constructed view of understanding taste. Participant 3, with whom I conducted an in-person interview, noted that playing the game "makes [him] realize that perhaps [his] musical taste is not as mainstream as what most people like. ... Perhaps my playlist does not have a lot of mainstream music that the normal, the average Joe, will have on their playlist. That's what it made me conscious of." Much of this point echoes Bourdieu's operation of distinctions whereby he argued that people were in fear of being ordinary; although this participant did not particularly express pride in his tastes, it was clear that his own reflections allowed him to construct his identity as being different from others.

Another aspect of the game involved learning about what one liked, independent of others' tastes. In other words, the game functioned as a way to discover what music one liked and disliked, and at the end of the game, the website automatically saved the music one liked and created a playlist at the bottom of the game. As Participant 1 stated, "No more or less, I feel like I can find out about different music through it as well."

In addition to determining one's musical preferences, participants also mentioned that the game was a new means to discover music that they may not have been exposed to otherwise.

Learned anything? I'm not sure I can say that I learned anything. I may have; some music has come to my attention that I would like to give a listen to. I guess that counts as learning. So learning about other artists, or becoming aware of other artists and certain songs that came across the Hit or Not game, yes, I would say. (Participant 4)

Clearly, Hit or Not functions as a marketing and promotional tool for Warner Music Group artists, as participants are being introduced to WMG albums through this interactive game.

A minor discrepancy and confusion existed when several participants mentioned that some of the songs that were considered "hits" in previous years were not considered hits by today's game players. Participants who were old enough to recall music from the previous decades applied their own knowledge of hit music from a factual standpoint rather than playing the game based on their own tastes. One woman, who had played the game while her daughter passively observed, noted how some people who played the game have recreated the musical standard in terms of the hit factor.

For instance, my daughter was staying there going, "Well, that's a hit," even though it said it wasn't. A lot of the songs were hits a long time ago, in their day when they were a hit, but it said they weren't. I don't think it was really true, but it depends on who's listening to it, though. (Participant 12)

Another participant also stated that he was confused by how tastes were conceived differently according to different time periods:

What's confusing about the game is there are tunes that they play that are hits that people don't like, that are scored not a hit. Basically I know that because of my experience, I know that the song was a Top 40 hit in 1999 or whatever. ... The game really isn't realistic. (Participant 9)

Participant 3 echoed this point:

A lot of the more younger generation I think modify rather than some of the old school people. When you come across *Ray of Light* by Madonna, and it was very popular back when it was released in 1998. It reached number five on the Billboard chart. It was not popular [in the game].

Maybe the people that did not rate that popular, maybe they're more into Lady Gaga. If there's a Lady Gaga, Madonna. Maybe they're more into the mainstream but now, whereas Madonna is not as mainstream as she was back then. It could be that a more progressive, younger generation that was not really exposed to 1998 Madonna, was rating it low. Whereas maybe the percentage of the country that liked *Ray of Light* maybe were older Spotify users.

In this context, the game has shed new light, to some users, on the transient nature of music's popularity as it relates to historical and cultural time periods. Simultaneously, the game showed potential through the reevaluation efforts of the players. In this process, the game defies past songs' perceived popularity and operates through collectively re-creating the musical tastes and values of the present time.

Discussion

Drawing on these exploratory findings, three emerging themes were noteworthy in understanding the game's purpose, uses, and further implications as they relate to the evaluation process: (1) the new type of market research and advertising, (2) the gamification of evaluation, and (3) learning about personal versus collective tastes in music. While we may need more substantive empirical data to draw a solid conclusion, as far as the findings from this study are concerned, the music evaluation methods are flawed and problematic on several grounds. There is a potential danger in this evaluation game in influencing evaluators to adopt a certain type of assessment criteria: instead of recognizing a variety of ways in which music can be experienced, appreciated, and liked, the game imposes only one way to evaluate music. Is a song a hit or not? Furthermore, the music evaluation game runs on the logic of gamification, but this creates conflicts of interests. According to Nicholson (2012), "The underlying concept of gamification is motivation" (1). If the players are motivated to win, this goal may potentially skew the evaluation process, because game players are rewarded for guessing hit songs regardless of how one evaluates the game. However, because the players noted that they were not motivated to win, despite the flawed rationale behind the evaluation game, the evaluation surprisingly did not result in any skewed or misleading judgments. Rather, the leading factors in the evaluation process were personal opinions about a particular song and the players' guesses in alignment or opposition with others' predictions.

While it would be easy to view the game as a reinforcement of the capitalistic ethos, one of the game's unique features is its potential to re-create various standards of music or popularity by the select participants. The puzzlement that some users expressed about previous hit music being considered unpopular has several implications. On the one hand, the game shows that most songs' popularity is transient, although some songs are considered "classics." This status may have more to do with the social and cultural imposition of a song becoming "classic" than with listeners' ongoing preferences regardless of generation and age. Furthermore, tastes are clearly shaped in relation to the time period and sentiments of a specific era. To this extent, there is room to exercise human agency and empowerment, even in a seemingly problematic and flawed evaluation game such as this one.

Finally, the social psychological dimension was noteworthy. While keeping in mind that this research is a pilot study, the findings from the interviewees' comments indicate that hardly any participants were affected or influenced by others' musical tastes, unlike previous research findings that reflect a symbiosis between social and peers' influence and the shaping of musical standard.

Limitations and Future Research Directions

Although the seventeen survey participants' contributions to my study were invaluable in providing preliminary insights on emerging issues, further research should explore a variety of issues presented here. The participants for this research were all adults, eighteen and older; it would be interesting to analyze the potentially different experiences of a younger audience group. The same point was also echoed by Participant 2 in noting how the game encouraged young people to be competitive:

Yeah, I think younger ... maybe like an eight-year-old would be interested in that kind of competition. I don't think an adult would be like, "Hey, I'm ahead of you on Hit or Not today." It's weird. The page just came up and ... I know I had points, but I'm down to zero points. I don't know if they wipe the points off when they changed the name to Hit or Not.

If this game could potentially motivate and entertain young players, it would be worthwhile to examine how young players might approach the game. Given a strong correlation between youth peer pressure and connections with music and identity formation (Selfhout, Branje, ter Bogt, and Meeus 2009), the implications of the game may be more alarming if this age group's musical tastes are heavily affected by their peers and a desire to "fit in."

Another limitation in the study was the length of playing time, which was approximately thirty minutes for new users who had never played the game before. It is unclear whether the participants actually spent thirty minutes playing, as this could not be checked or verified. Furthermore, although a minimum of thirty minutes was supposedly sufficient to get acquainted with the game, many people still showed confusion. The research outcomes might have differed if the participants had played the game longer. For this reason, a longitudinal study could be of value to discern the impact of the game on the individual formation of musical tastes and evaluation standards. Does playing the game over a long-term period shift one's evaluation standards in music? If so, how?

A lack of interest in the game overall could also serve as a limitation. Hit or Not is not yet a prominent cultural phenomenon by any means. It may be a fleeting, experimental application, although, according to the 2013 Digital Music Report, Spotify is a rapidly growing streaming site worldwide and is touted as having the most potential to grow (IFPI 2013). In this context, the trajectory of the game's future could go either way; it may become more prominent or die sooner than expected. The Facebook Hit or Not page has disappeared, and this development may foreshadow this application's demise, indicating that the game may not have met the expectations of Spotify and Warner Music Group.

Finally, the findings for this study are all based on self-reporting, and we cannot ignore the aspect that there can be personal bias since these individuals may not want to admit that they are easily influenced by others; thus, future research should take into consideration ways to mitigate potential bias created by the users.

Overall, taking into account an in-depth analysis of the game's motivations, underlying premises, and reward system, as well as the participants' in-depth interviews, we can characterize this evaluation game as an ironic juxtaposition of simplicity and complexity. Although the game is one-dimensional and overly simple, the underlying motives and logistics of the game and its rewards are layered in ideological, sociological, historical, and personal contexts.

3 Evaluations of Music by Peers and Professionals on Indaba Music

Introduction

Music evaluations have often been fraught with controversy. Inasmuch as generating a consensus about music's value and quality has been challenging and contentious, the various methods, criteria, and standards related to music's qualitative value have been underexplored, if not generally ignored, in the discipline of cultural studies.

Echoing this observation, Frith (1996) notes that "the importance of value judgment for popular culture ... seems obvious, but it has been quite neglected in academic cultural studies" (8). This neglect deserves to be studied more carefully because, with the rise of digital media, the evaluation methods for music are constantly evolving. For instance, during Myspace's heyday, the number of "friends" that musicians had on their profiles undoubtedly played a dominant role in launching the professional careers of various popular music artists (Suhr 2012). Other sites, such as YouTube, continue to be forceful factors in musicians' careers, since the value of musicians is often determined by the number of views their videos receive. Despite some concerns about the impact of music contests on the productivity and value of music (Miller 1994), competitions and contests are ubiquitous in digital environments, where they influence the rankings and hierarchies connected with the value and popularity of works produced by both amateur and professional musicians. Overall, digital environments have become a *contested terrain*, echoing Warf and Grimes's (1997) view that "the Internet is neither inherently oppressive nor automatically emancipatory; it is a terrain of contested philosophies and politics" (259). In this context, the goal of this chapter is to unpack the shifting landscape of music evaluation in the digital era by focusing on musicians' general views of peer assessments, voting, and experts' criticism on Indaba Music.

Indaba Music

Indaba Music launched its website in 2007, and as of 2014, this online community boasts more than eight hundred thousand musician members. As a for-profit company, Indaba Music currently offers three types of memberships. A basic membership allows musicians to enter three opportunities per year for free and comes with 200 MB of storage, while a pro membership, $5 a month, grants five opportunities per month and 5 GB of storage. For $25 a month, the platinum membership provides unlimited opportunities and 50 GB of storage. On its Creative Commons blog, Indaba Music explains that artists can choose either to reserve all rights or to sign a Creative Commons license, which gives permission for specified uses of their work by others (Parkins 2008).

Shortly after the birth of Indaba Music, the site held many contests that involved remixing already established popular musicians' new releases. A survey of Indaba Music's contest archives from 2012 to 2013 reveals that its contests quickly proliferated, and now there are many new types of contests on the site. While remix contests continue to be prominent, other types of unique opportunities range from educational to strictly work-for-hire situations that provide music for particular genres or soundtracks for varieties of media. In return, contest winners received monetary rewards and different types of exposure.

For instance, contests such as Et Musique Pour Tous generate opportunities to interact with new types of cultural intermediaries. According to the Indaba Music site, "Et Musique Pour Tous is a music and culture blog dedicated to quality, not traffic. It has built a reputation as being influential amongst music supervisors and other tastemakers." To this end, the reward was additional exposure, which served as a seal of approval, to some extent. Similarly, the Electronica Oasis contest asked musicians to submit original electronic dance music for the opportunity to be interviewed and featured on the popular Electronica Oasis music blog. The blog boasts thousands of visitors a month, and Indaba Music noted that the site has "become a go-to destination for electronic dance music lovers to get their fix." In March 2013, Artist Search gave its winner the opportunity to have Indaba Music produce a record. The Emerging Artist contest awarded the chosen musician with studio time in either Los Angeles or New York City and gear from the Blue Microphones. In addition, Music Xray invited musicians to submit music for evaluation by the music industry in terms of potential fan appeal. Thus far, I have highlighted only select examples to showcase how widely varied the contests are on Indaba Music, but note that as many as twenty-nine contests may be going on within a given month.

Not only has the number of contests increased, but some offer opportunities for professional development with industry insiders, such as Grammy U: The Masters' Critique. This contest was unique in that the contest finalists had the opportunity to meet industry professionals in person to gain advice and feedback on their music; in a sense, the competition operated as a professional career coaching session. With a focus on the expanding scope of Indaba Music's contests, the next section analyzes the emergence of peer assessments, as well as professional industry critics, and how these may potentially aid and hinder informal learning experiences for musicians.

Evaluations, Rating, and Ranking on Indaba Music

The effort to distinguish and rank musicians has not diminished since the heyday of the Billboard charts and rankings, but the metric has been reconfigured for social media. A case in point is the inclusion of YouTube ranking in the Billboard charts (Sisario 2013), as well as the introduction of the Social 50 chart that tracks popularity emerging from social media (Billboard.com). Although it no longer exists, BBC's Sound Index used to be a comprehensive evaluation mechanism that accounted for multiple types of data, such as the number of listens, plays, downloads, sales, and comments (Bhagwan et al. 2009).

As such, the evaluation mechanisms in social media have adopted the format of the charts from the mainstream industry. The need to order and rank music online is imperative owing to the decentralized nature of digital environments. No longer can one consider music produced online as only amateur or leisure productions, since many of these activities are pursued by amateurs on the verge of becoming professionals. To this extent, digital environments hold enormous power in the ordering process that prioritizes musicians into a newly emerging hierarchy. One of the ways in which this organization takes place is through contests. Yet unlike other formats of social media charts, where the criteria are often based on a simple measure of views, plays, likes, or friends, Indaba Music's system is slightly different, as the site allows winners to be selected by industry or genre experts, while peers, along with algorithms, play the role of gatekeepers before the final outcome. To further contextualize the Indaba Music community's evaluation systems, the concept of cultural intermediaries needs to be explored.

The Emergence of Peer and Professional Critics

In digital environments, newly emerging cultural intermediaries include a variety of people. Unlike the previous category of cultural intermediaries (i.e., the mass consumers who stepped in to raise popularity and recognitions), the activities of professional critics collide with peer opinions on Indaba Music. Negus (2002) first recognized the expanding scope of cultural intermediaries, and today Indaba Music proves that evaluations are no longer being generated solely by select people of influence and power but are being produced by four different types of people: professionals, peers, cultural producers' personal networks, and everyday consumers.

In a similar vein, Lieb (2013) discusses the role of niche gatekeepers, who exist "in the form of bloggers, podcasters, Facebook friends, and song and album recommenders on iTunes and Amazon" (79). Lieb notes that despite these newly emerging gatekeepers, "conventional music industry gatekeepers are still abundant and powerful in the role of building and popularizing artists and music" (79). Much of this claim is true. Although Indaba Music specifically includes the peer critic as part of its group of cultural intermediaries, the primary attraction to the site and its contests is potential connections with the traditional gatekeepers in the music industry, according to survey participants.

Lieb (2013) further elaborates on the emergence of cultural intermediaries, from both the production and the consumption sides. On the consumption side, the gatekeepers include radio station owners, programmers, and television station and film owners and producers. It is noteworthy that previously gatekeepers influenced the type of music that consumers were exposed to through a tight control of access as arbitrated by A&R and business executives (Frith 2000). However, in the digital era, consumers increasingly seek their own gatekeepers, individuals whom they trust on social networking sites and music sites:

> [The] new niche of gatekeepers has the potential to dilute the power of the traditional gatekeepers by showing artists that there are new ways of attracting a following and becoming popular without them. But still, those interviewed could not come up with examples of significant artists who had broken big without the support of traditional gatekeepers, which itself is telling data. (Lieb 2013, 80)

As revealed by Lieb, in the digital era, niche cultural intermediaries and traditional cultural intermediaries are acting not independently but collaboratively. Given that commercial success (as in "breaking big") is still ultimately aided by conventional gatekeepers, the older power structures persist. This is a critical point to remember, since the intricate interplay between the traditional gatekeepers and niche gatekeepers inevitably has symbiotic effects, although different interests are at stake (i.e., for mainstream artists, the promotion and marketing of new releases from the labels; on the other hand, grassroots artists seek opportunities for work and exposure). To this end, it is not surprising that a site like Indaba Music attracts musicians, as many opportunities center on collaboration with a variety of traditional and niche gatekeepers. While traditional gatekeepers are present, Indaba Music mainly operates as a niche gatekeeper. With this idea in mind, I would like to demarcate another category of "subniche gatekeepers," comprising peer critics on music websites. In the case of Indaba Music, the subniche gatekeepers are the musicians who compete on the site while also serving as initial gatekeepers for other users, driving much of the traffic to the site and creating buzz.

In my previous research on Indaba Music, I explored the Yo-Yo Ma contest as a case study; one of the prominent themes related to that contest was the problematic voting system among contestants (Suhr 2012). Now, a few years later, Indaba Music's contests continue to face the same problem in regard to voting and popularity. While my previous research data were gathered by conducting a textual analysis of the discussion forum on the actual content site, this study incorporates surveys from 255 participants, nonexclusive to any particular contest, and includes interviews and a textual analysis of Indaba Music's massive contest archives (but with particular attention to 2012 and 2013). In light of this study, I have explored the mixed responses about peer assessments.

Peer Assessments and Informal Critiques on Indaba Music

While Indaba Music's finalists are chosen by a rotating panel of select judges (often professionals in the music industry or Indaba Music staff), peer assessments are also an integral part of the contests. Understanding how peers assess one another's work has long been an interest of music education researchers (Blom and Poole 2004; Hunter 1999; Lebler 2008). The benefits of learning from other peers have been studied, in particular, by Jones and King (2009), who illustrate how this can be achieved in a recording studio through "surrogate teaching" and "proctoring."

Increasingly, social media platforms and new media technologies for alternative music pedagogy have attracted the interest of music educators and researchers alike (Rudolph and Frankel 2009; Chong 2011; Ruthmann 2007; Waldron and Veblen 2008). For Burnard (2007), "technologically mediated music making can shake the most cherished practices of classroom music teachers—but on the other hand, it can generate the desire to (and ways in which to) diversify existing pedagogical practice" (39). In this vein, previous studies focused on the characteristics of amateur criticism of YouTube music performances (Suhr 2008) and on the nature of YouTube music video commenting (Thelwall, Sud, and Vis 2012). These studies show how digital platforms can be active places for discussing musical quality and performances, for expressing personal tastes, and for reviewing performances in an informal context. Although these platforms are limited in space and are rarely influential beyond the websites themselves, they are useful places for music listeners to exercise their informal critiques and to share their tastes. Other platforms also exist, and they elevate the informal critique to a professional context, one that is significant to music industry insiders.

Despite strengths in peer mentoring and a variety of ways in which informal criticisms are practiced on social networking sites, peer assessments in the context of reputation mechanisms raise concern. Marti and Garcia-Molina (2006) posit that peer-to-peer reputation systems include the consideration of incentives and punishment, and Papaioannou and Stamoulis (2006) focus on the issue of exploiting reputations: "It appears that a high-performing peer is thus unfairly 'punished'" (565). In noting this bias and inequality, the authors problematize how these "incentives lead to a market of 'lemons' and possibly to the gradual collapse of the peer to peer system" (565).

Similar trends were also noted on Indaba Music regarding the influence of peers in building one's reputation. Although the voting procedures do not determine the winners, voting has some merit, since through this process, musicians gain additional exposure during the contests and may end up receiving honorable mentions. It is noteworthy that ascribing value takes place through hype generated within the community. Musicians often describe the problematic nature of peer assessment. One user, who had been received positively during a contest, also pointed out the bias during the judgment process:

As an individual who has received Honorable Mentions and success on the Indaba website, I can say without bias that the tracks on this site which receive the most acknowledgement are not the deserving tracks, but the ones that are marketed the most sufficiently. Also the winners are chosen not by trained judges who base their opinions and decisions on multiple sets of established criteria, but merely the subjective opinion of the artist who is the Judge for each particular contest. (Indaba survey)

In addition to the issue of voting and tireless marketing, the commentator noted the role played by arbitrary taste in determining the winners.

On Indaba Music, the system by which musicians are ranked is based on multiple measurements, such as how many peers have taken interest in listening to and critiquing fellow contestants. Any Indaba member can listen, comment, and provide feedback. Nonetheless, contrary to the common belief that feedback on music by peer musicians should be helpful, many musicians stated that feedback was only a means to an end, not an end unto itself. In short, positive feedback was given with the expectation of reciprocity; many peers were serving as what Hearn (2010) calls "feeling intermediaries," whose goals are to give and receive positive feedback.

A lot of musicians on Indaba go around spamming (leaving good comments on other people's songs while politely asking for good comments back). I've seen lots and lots of really bad and mediocre music placing itself as a hot track and in the leader board because of this system and it's ridiculous and not fair that musicians get ranked by their own rivals. On the other hand I think the songs chosen by the judges as winners of the contest are always very deserved, so I think there should be no popular vote winner and all the winners should be chosen by the judges. (Indaba survey)

In this context, being candid with one's criticism or feedback often does not seem feasible, because peers fear that it could potentially have a negative impact on their own competitions.

There is no way one will get honest feedback on their songs because, as we depend on votes from our peers and if we have negative critics for someone, they are unlikely to vote for us. Therefore the whole commenting experience becomes insincere, sugar-coated BS. (Indaba survey)

Although there is a growing concern over the inauthentic nature of peer feedbacks, not all comments can be viewed as nonconstructive criticisms. Some survey participants argued that Indaba Music's competitions had some learning value, insofar as one could gain a better appreciation of individual fortes and areas in need of improvement: "Hearing competition give[s] oneself a good understanding of where one's strengths and weakness are" (Indaba survey). The other useful aspect was the chance to learn about professional-quality sound and mixing techniques: "It is a great opportunity for me to learn a lot more about production and mixing by analyzing and working with the commercial tracks provided in the contests" (Indaba survey). Another participant noted, "Constructive critiques can have a positive impact on music. I have used other sites that offer feedback and when it is good it is usually accepted. When it's not it is questioned or disregarded" (Indaba survey). Although not all the survey comments stated that peer feedback is meaningless, the prominent trend was still based on giving positive feedback for reciprocity. At this juncture, it would be worthwhile to consider how online critiques from peers compared to expert criticisms in the Indaba Music contest Grammy U: The Masters' Critique.

Grammy U: The Masters' Critique

To further understand informal learning in a contest setting, I conducted a case study on Grammy U: The Masters' Critique. According to the Grammy 365 website, Grammy U is a "fast-growing community of college students, primarily between the ages of 17 and 25, who are pursuing a career in the recording industry." The goal of Grammy U is to offer students an "out of classroom" experience, replicating real professional industry experience. Grammy U was held to provide direct critical feedback from professionals in the music industry. The contest took place in April 2012, and the contestants were asked to submit one song each. The chosen finalists and one winner were invited to a live finale at the Recording Academy in New York City. They also received oral and written critiques of their submissions from a panel of music industry professionals. The opportunity for aspiring musicians to be heard by professionals in the music industry is extremely valuable. Since many musicians hope to become professionals, the stakes were high for many contestants.

With this understanding of the contest and its stakes, I set forth a research process to assess the learning aspect tied to the competition framework. In addition to a textual analysis of the discussion forums of the Grammy U contest, I also interviewed five finalists by telephone and had a face-to-face conversation with the contest winner. For the purposes of this study, the finalists were all assigned random numbers without any specific meaning or organization, to retain their anonymity.

The five finalists all discussed how this opportunity helped them better understand their strengths and weaknesses as musicians. Yet an interesting difference between traditional critiques by critics and professionals and those by amateurs emerged here. Traditionally, music critics served to "take on the role of denouncing the new in the name of old" (Frith 2002, 236). In short, the role of critics was often to unpack difficult music for nonprofessional listeners; in doing so, many critics leaned toward the valorization of musicality and originality. In contrast, the informal critiques that took place during the Grammy U competition were slightly different in focus, since the critics mainly concentrated on helping the competitors hone their sound to correspond with popular preferences:

What they were telling me was to make it more. Make it, maybe change up the lyrics so that more people can relate to. Or change up the stylish production or get new producer so that it will be radio hit. You know with like the electric, electro pop scene. ... They kind of told to be like you can't go that way. But ultimately it's your choice because it's my song. I believe. Well I can't say 100 percent for like the radio hits or like the top songs, but ... it's for like the catchier purpose or for the purpose being more audible to more listeners. (Finalist 2)

Finalist 4 also noted that the "critique was definitely hit song focused" but concluded that the judges were aware that not every artist was interested in creating a hit song. In citing one of the judges, Finalist 4 mentioned that the advice given was not to compromise one's style as an artist and that all the opinions should be taken with a grain of salt. Finalist 5 made a similar point:

> For example, they really stressed that songs should be, especially for ones that you want to have played on the radio, they should be very short and concise and you don't have any unnecessary solos or filler at all. We actually were pleasantly surprised by the fact that we kept our songs really short and to the point. The people at Grammy U, they listened to each of the songs while all the finalists were in the room, and they only played them for something like two and half minutes or three minutes of the song. They said that's what a generous producer or PR person would actually listen to if a song got submitted to them.

The opportunity provided for these finalists pertained to learning the formula for writing a catchy tune that could potentially turn into a hit song. Nonetheless, as Finalist 5 noted, even if his goals were not aligned with being a hit songwriter, these critiques held value for him.

The motivation for entering the contest is also an important factor in understanding what these musicians were aiming to get out of the experience. Finalist 2 entered "to get my music out there for people to listen or for anyone. Not even industry professionals. Just for anyone to take a listen to my song." The interviewee noted that entering the contest was an "eye-opening" experience, since he learned that industry professionals also liked his song. This served as a seal of approval, which resulted in him feeling inspired to "continue to pursue music as a professional." This finalist also mentioned how the opportunity had helped him learn about the songwriting process. The judges' constructive criticism of his music was invaluable, in part because of their varying backgrounds. When Finalist 2 compared the contest to his musical education in a formal university setting, he claimed that the experiences were not strikingly different: "At least what my school teaches is how to become a very good overall musician, and it's the very same aspect of what they told me as the feedback on my song."

Additionally, there was the intrinsic reward that comes from sharing one's music. "Well, like all musicians, everyone wants their stuff heard. I truly entered the contest, one, I wanted to get my message across saying this is my music, and this is what I need to say to the world, and I hope I inspire one of you guys" (Finalist 2). Another major extrinsic motivator for entering the contest was to make connections within the music industry:

I want to make connections because I want to become a professional, or I want to become a successful musician, and so far I'm just a student. I believe that this is a good head start. I really don't mind about how many badges I have. I don't really mind about those badges. They could take them off and I don't—I wouldn't mind. (Finalist 2)

As clearly evinced here, badges were neither the ultimate goal nor a primary interest; rather, Finalist 2's goal was to clearly learn how to become a professional musician.

Finalist 3, however, gave a slightly different account of what he learned through the critiquing process.

No, I don't think I learned too much about our music in particular. ... They each gave their perspective say on things. They kind of told us about it, but it wasn't anything that we haven't heard yet, you know what I mean?

This person further noted that the professional critique suggested niche markets into which the finalists' music could fit. Finalist 3 was told that his type of music would do better in Europe's hip-hop scene, but this musician desired more concrete advice on how to launch his career. Besides comments about his music's viability and marketability, he also received criticism about the technical aspects of his production. The engineer on the panel constructively commented that he would prefer to have the sound of the snare be more prominent in the mix. Finalist 3 also mentioned that some of the critiques were contradictory in nature.

The one singer, her critique was contradicting. She said, the first guy was very playful and she likes to have a little bit more raw of rapper, and then the second rapper on that song, she criticized him for being a little too raw. I don't think she knew too much about hip-hop or this or that. She kind of contradicted herself because the song consisted of about four rappers, and I made the beat and recorded it, so that's pretty much what it was. It was kind of tough for her to give anything feedback wise because we didn't have any singing, except for samples that are put in there.

Finalist 3 noted that in addition to learning where his music might sell well, he was interested in learning about specific avenues and recommendations about where to go and what to do to take his career to the next level. For this finalist, receiving feedback from professionals was not necessarily the most beneficial thing, because he felt that anonymous feedback could give a real measure of how his music is being received by the audience. In referring to one of the sites that performs such analysis (Sound-Out), he said, "That has probably been the best feedback that I've gotten because you've got to base yourself on what normal people out there walking on the streets think about your music. Somebody who likes country but hates hip hop and they're forced to write something about this."

Finally, in the interview with the contest winner, I was interested in learning if he might have perceived the experience differently. His goal for entering the contest was no different from the others' goals, as his main motivation was to become a professional musician. Besides the Grammy U contest, he had competed in other contests and had earned some positive outcomes and recognition. In speaking about his other motivations, he mentioned a desire to "broaden [his] skill" beyond performance, specifically referencing remixing and film compositions. Although he noted that the competition may further his career as a performing artist, it brought with it other benefits, such as getting involved in "things that are outside of that immediate niche." He mentioned that winning the competition was "like a portfolio expander." Although he already had quite a number of badges, he was not even aware of them until I pointed them out. Given this ignorance, it was clear that badges were neither his goal nor his interest.

As for the rewards from winning the contest, he mentioned that he was supposed to get a free recording session, as well as an opportunity to have a conversation with various record label executives. Although the advertised rewards were pending at the time of our interview, the winner noted that he had already received other rewards because of his win. Overall, he seemed rather indifferent about receiving the rewards because, outside of the Indaba Music network, he was in discussion with a label about a record deal. This was similar to the experience of another musician I interviewed. He too had been involved with Indaba Music, but his recent publishing deal came through another site called SoundCloud; through that platform, someone randomly approached him and invited him to present his work to be considered for a publishing deal. For many musicians, Indaba Music is just one opportunity out of an array of similar ones, such as the opportunities on paramountsong.com, unsigned-only music competitions, and international songwriting contests. Indaba

Music does not seem to be their inevitable choice if they are trying to further their career paths.

Nonetheless, the winner claimed that entering the contest provided a valuable learning opportunity, since it allowed him to hear other people's music and divergent approaches to making music. He mentioned that it "forces him out of [his] comfort zone," and he considers that to be one of its major benefits:

I find the feedback useful. Whether or not I apply it, it's always good to hear because people who love you don't necessarily always give you that kind of critical feedback. People who don't love you don't give you anything useful ... because you feel defensive or something. Authority figures are dangerous but sometimes they are the only ones who can provide something.

Feedback given by professional critics is valuable but clearly does not necessarily change one's direction in music. This point was also echoed by others who felt that criticisms are only of limited usefulness; as such, the musicians do not uncritically accept them as either right or wrong, just as advisory.

The other rewards from this opportunity related to building a reputation as an artist. The winner believed that he could get more exposure to industry professionals as a result of winning and becoming more recognizable in the community.

The best I could say is that in the Grammy U critique it was by ... The critique was by pretty mysterious people, all four of whom now know who I am. That doesn't give me any tangible benefits, but the next time they hear my name it'll be the second time; that counts for something. The third time they hear my name they'll be like, "Why do I keep hearing this guy's name?" That's how things happen.

Much of the reward for entering this contest and winning was measured by the winner in terms of the long-term benefit of creating a buzz among industry professionals.

Taken as a whole, learning through digital platforms has its pros and cons; while these environments clearly mitigate the proximity between professionals in the music industry and aspiring musicians who seek opportunities in the music business, the learning experience is directly linked to understanding what is desired by the commercial music industry professionals. This dimension can be received positively as well as negatively, depending on one's ideological stance and allegiance. Given the long-standing tension between art and commerce, on the one hand, one may argue that these musicians are being trained to write only hit songs. On the other hand, one may claim that this is a highly useful opportunity, as musicians whose goals are to become working musicians in the music business would find this similar to real-world experiences. Many of the implications of learning here intersect with the discussions on the commercialism of music. Yet it is worth pointing out that these contestants did not necessarily take all the advice at face value. While Finalist 4 had thought about following through on some of the recommendations about making a radio hit (i.e., a shorter, catchy tune), other finalists were more selective in what they were willing to change.

As for understanding how these experiences might bridge the conventional educational context, some of the finalists who are music students did not find the experience drastically different from their academic activities. As universities often employ professors who have a professional background in music, the finalists felt that what was being taught inside and outside the classroom was complementary, rather than a totally new avenue of approach.

Overall, it seems that digital environments have opened up wider opportunities for musicians to learn in diverse contexts, allowing for learning from peers and random listeners, as well as professionals. Rather than representing an alternative way to learn, the digital environment seems to function in tandem with classroom learning experiences. The only major difference is the emphasis on the professional development of musicians in the digital environments. It is not necessary to polarize these experiences into a moral stance of good or bad, but it is up to musicians to decide what pathway they plan on taking. Most importantly, although the critiques from industry professionals were limited in their impact, the musicians themselves believed that the experience was valuable, not because they will ultimately change their styles but because it increased their understanding of the standards and expectations of the professional music industry.

Toward the Challenges of Building an Ideal Music Evaluation Process

Research in the realm of music contests has already noted the shortcomings of competitions in relation to music pedagogy (Austin 1990). In particular, Glejser and Heyndels (2001) observed a discrepancy in evaluation results in terms of the ranking order of musicians. A similar observation was made by Haan, Dijkstra, and Dijkstra (2005), noting that musicians who perform later in contests ranked better than earlier contestants, thus pointing out the bias and inefficiency in the system. Moreover, the issues with competitions are not exclusive to popular genres of music. Classical music competitions echo the problematic nature of evaluations, confirming the findings connected with Indaba Music. In her observation of classical music contests, McCormick (2009) notes three major findings from the contestants: (1) "Competitions are inherently arbitrary and unfair," (2) "competitions failed to discover the next generation of great artist," and (3) "competitions had actually done more harm than good" (13–14). While there is a clear difference between classical offline contests and online contests, which predominately focus on driving traffic to the sites in question, the first conclusion was echoed by many Indaba musicians. In this regard, the issue was not just who should be the judge of music, or if one should solely blame the corporate system that credentializes musicians for profit; the main underlying question pertains to whether music can be judged in a fair, objective way at all. In the case of music, the issues of subjectivity of tastes and aesthetic standards present serious challenges to establishing fair criteria and assessment systems:

Everything is based on the judges in these contests and how open they are to new ideas for the winner. The rest of the winners are subjective to how many places they link their songs with. So the people with more computer time have a better audience for the votes. (Indaba survey)

In general, musicians find that when it comes to evaluations of music, neither the quantity of popular votes nor the evaluations by the judges fully indicated a work's value. The issues brought up by most musicians were related to the subjectivity of tastes.

It is impossible to rank, rate or evaluate music from the beginning. Accuracy, justice and so on on this matter is pointless to talk about. However, these still are contests we are talking about. Someone has to win, but it does not mean it is the best music created. It was just the right piece for the judges. (Indaba survey)

Another survey participant echoed the earlier comment, albeit more philosophically:

Sound doesn't exist, it's just vibrations, with that said it's my brain telling me if the music is good or not. It's all down to one's subconscious, memory will also play a major role. So it's down to that one individual and that one piece of music at that given point in time. (Indaba survey)

Music was also perceived not as a form of commodity but rather in affective terms, tapping into the personal interior: "Good music is something that comes from the heart that resonates with people who are listening to it. It evokes a feeling of calm, gratitude, happiness or is a catharsis of some sort" (Indaba survey). Another survey recipient replied:

One person's love is another person's hate. Music allows freedom of expression, which is a good thing. The best part of music is that like art, it is up to each individual to decide for themselves what is good. Unfortunately this freedom is also why a lot of talented people miss out on getting recognition for their work.

The subjectivity of musical standards was echoed by many members: "Music is subjective. It usually tells us what the judges were looking for, and how to gain votes in the future" (Indaba survey). Another musician noted: "There is no such thing as 'universal criteria' when it comes to an inherently subjective art. Anyone who says otherwise is either misinformed—or an asshole" (Indaba survey).

One musician commented that even when the judges make a decision, the judges' own perceptions about good music are flawed and biased because they themselves are influenced by how the public is reacting to a track.

Well, we can't speak of fairness when the criteria is completely subjective. Although I suspect that the judges often make decisions based on what they *think* [the] general public will like rather than on what "good" music is. As for the contests decided by votes—those are completely skewed towards people with most friends/connections. (Indaba survey)

Overall, many of the Indaba musicians' survey responses reveal the perception that music evaluative metrics are inherently flawed and biased. Are we moving toward a crisis of evaluations? Is music evaluation based on contests or competitions at an impasse?

Conclusion

In this chapter, I have explored several ways in which musicians are evaluated. In doing so, I delineated some emerging problems, as well as potential benefits, connected to criticisms and learning opportunities that proliferate on Indaba Music. Although peer evaluations were an integral part of the site's activities, this process of evaluation turned into social protocols and mechanical reciprocity. As these mechanisms faltered and complaints about popular votes soared, Indaba Music reacted. In the summer of 2013, Indaba Music attempted to rectify the problematic voting methods. The leaderboard, a section on the contest site where contestants can view the progress of their votes, now exhibits the sources of the votes: Is a vote coming from Indaba (peers) or from networks of random Facebook friends? Through this demarcation, the leaderboard tracks the origins of popularity. This modification reveals that digital environments are often dynamic in nature; they can be modified over time, although it is unclear whether the changes will always lead to improvement.

While awareness is the first step toward a remedy, the musicians from these sites illustrate that they are more than capable of assessing the evaluation systems based on their own experiences. As one interviewee insightfully puts it, judgments and evaluations are, in essence, operating as "quality control" (Indaba Musician 1, personal communication with author). By and large, many of the comments from the survey reflect incisive personal critiques, which subsequently prompted the researcher to focus on their messages. Yet the challenges of critiquing the evaluation of works of art not only lie in the system itself but also point to the inherent problems that underlie the subjectivity of musical and aesthetic tastes. Of course, this does not mean that the developers or the owners of these sites are innocent of attempts at exploitation. However, along with the continual problematization of evaluation methods through an active construction of scholarly discourses, we should also explore creative producers' goals and intrinsic pleasures and gains, especially in light of Amabile's (1996) argument that intrinsic rewards generally improve the levels of creativity, while external rewards mitigate creativity. The impetus for competing may not be based on fair evaluation systems. Nonetheless, learning experiences and intrinsic pleasures are also part of the experience. Musicians on Indaba Music often attributed the broken system, the luck- and chance-based evaluation, to both internal politics and the game of subjectivity. Yet this is not surprising if we recall the other means to evaluate music (i.e., moral systems, aesthetic experiences) that contradict the common conception of music as commodified cultural goods. In short, as the evaluation of music proliferates in the digital era, the specific context as well as multiple and transient factors that affect the shaping of criteria and standard should also be considered.

4 Underpinning Digital Badges as a Symbol of Honor

In the resentment and dissonance that musicians often express toward applying popularity as a standard for assessing music, it is clear that alternative credentialing methods are necessary. Yet many musicians are skeptical of what the new criteria should be. In this chapter, I explore the potential for digital badges to offer an alternative credentialing means for building reputations.

Digital badges have recently emerged as an alternative credentialing system and have received increasing exposure in the media (Ash 2012; Lomas 2013). In its early stages, this system was explored through Mozilla's Open Badges program and the efforts of the Digital Media and Learning/HASTAC (Humanities, Arts, Technology and Science Alliance and Collaboratory), MacArthur Foundation. Goligoski (2012) explained in detail how the badges would be implemented. For instance, Mozilla would work with "career website and credentialing portfolio and profile system[s]," such as LinkedIn. Furthermore, when clicked, the badges would indicate what skill sets or accomplishments they represented. Overall, this system sought to bridge formal and informal learning frameworks, the underlying premise being that learning takes place over a lifetime, not just in school settings. Goligoski also noted public concerns ranging across a wide spectrum, but particularly related to confusion and a lack of unity or clarity of intent. A similar concern was expressed by Jenkins (2012) in his blog post "How to Earn Your Skeptic 'Badge,'" in which he highlighted some apprehensions about badges becoming a form of gamification, a means to earn points. He additionally questioned how the badges could have any uniformity of use and type. In a similar vein, Young (2012) discussed another potential concern with badges: "Badges turn all learning into a commodity and cheapen the difficult challenge of mastering something new" (50). Citing Cathy Davidson, a cofounding director of the digital learning network HASTAC, Young explained that one of the challenges connected to badges is a groundless prejudice toward their value and potential.

Although the research on digital badges is relatively new, the badges' potential merits have recently arisen as a topic of research with the active support of the Digital Media and Learning/HASTAC, MacArthur Foundation. So far, only a few articles have received attention in peer-reviewed journals. Halavais's (2012) comprehensive overview of the history of badges is noteworthy, as he describes the trajectory leading up to the digital era. Previously badges were often awarded for achievements and prestige, reflecting experience and group identification in their conveyance

In the context of education, Abramovich et al. (2013) demarcated the difference between educational badges and merit badges, such as those earned in video games. The authors noted how educational badges are for informal learners, and they highlighted the inevitable symbiosis in assessment and motivation. Much of the discussion of badges' benefits in educational learning environments was related to motivating students. How likely are students to be motivated to learn when they are being rewarded with badges? Drawing on findings taken from a group of thirty-six seventh graders and fifteen eighth graders at a charter school for teaching applied mathematics, Abramovich et al. (2013) noted that the motivational level for each student varied and depended on the different types of badges. Moreover, they noted that extrinsic motivators have a negative impact on learning.

Similarly, Rughiniş and Matei (2013) explored digital badges for their educational use, focusing specifically on two functions of badge architectures: "mapping a learning system and offering a vocabulary to present one's achievements" (1). The research indicates that badges operating within the intrinsic/extrinsic motivation dichotomy have conflicting results, and the authors proposed that badge architectures should be studied in light of their "descriptive and creative functions for the system in which they are implemented" (6). In line with this premise, this chapter thus aims to fill the gap that exists between the roles and functions of badges in educational contexts and in creative communities. To this end, I argue that rewards, motivations, and evaluations in creative communities pose differing types of challenges and complex intrinsic/extrinsic motivations. These must be confronted before the further development of the badge system can occur.

Digital Badges on Indaba Music

From the outset, let us distinguish between badges as a means to build reputation, honor, and prestige and badges as a means to showcase skill sets or mastery of a certain technique, such as mixing, producing, or engineering. The latter kind of badge functions similarly to the acquisition of licenses. Here my

inquiry extends beyond a simple identification of one's association and skill sets, since I am primarily interested in how
badges are used to enhance one's reputation, honor, and prestige. To understand the background rationale behind the inte-
gration of badges as part of Indaba Music, I interviewed Mantis
Evar, cofounder of Indaba Music. He explained that when the
site launched, it offered three different types of memberships:
basic, pro, and platinum. People were given three keys to unlock
opportunities taking place on the site; however, after they used
their three keys, although the site developer had expected the
members to upgrade their memberships to premium accounts,
many members would just "drop that profile and go create a
new one for free and get three more keys" (Evar interview). To
this extent, the keys were not generating revenue for the site, but
they did create a loophole in the system. To remedy the issue,
Evar told me, the Indaba team came up with a tool, "something
to be proud of ... to make their page something special."

Badges were developed as a way to ensure that members
would find their profile pages something to be "proud of." Evar
mentioned that when Indaba first started the badge system,
some members desired to purchase the badges:

They wanted special badges, they wanted to feel special. After explaining
to people that they didn't really need to purchase badges, that they were
something that was given out, it actually made me consider buyable
badges. Maybe something you can sell to buy for another member online. Almost like a fan badge. I love you, I want to buy a fan badge, I can
buy a fan badge. I came up with this idea of maybe for a dollar you buy
a fan badge; 50 percent of it goes to Indaba Music, the other 50 percent
goes to some sort of music charity or something. And so these fans are
working on supporting musicians, and also help support organizations
that could use a little extra support.

According to Evar's conversations with the members of Indaba Music, the members have valued the badges:

It means a lot for the people that are receiving the badges, whether it's given to them from Indaba Music, or whether they've earned it through a competition or something else. People seem to be very, very happy when they see another badge that pops up on their page. I have this one badge that we created called Music Appreciation Badge. And what this is is it's a badge for people that continue to give us positive input; their role: they're model members of the site. They work with each other, they communicate well. They are very active with our opportunities and stuff. And when we pull out these members, I personally give them those badges. And it's not something that you can work towards, it's something that is just rewarded because I know that, and I've been watching you, you are a great member, you've been supporting us all along, we love you, and here's an extra badge for you. (Evar interview)

Evar then described the evolution of the badges on Indaba Music. The first badge was called the Ninja badge. At the time, four Ninja badges were created for the cofounders of Indaba Music. Unlike most Indaba Music badges, which indicate their meaning if you point the cursor at them, the Ninja badge's meaning was kept hidden. Evar explained that many members wanted Ninja badges even though they did not know what the badges represented, because they were seen as something rare and very special. Now Indaba Music has many of these special badges, and their purpose is only revealed to members who receive them. Evar further explained how Indaba Music has come to categorize badges into four different groups: quality badges, association badges, activity badges, and specialty badges. He noted that people gain quality badges when they win a contest or are a runner-up, honorable mention, judges' pick, grand prize winner, or featured member. Association badges are given to Grammy U members who are part of the Grammy intern group.

After conducting my interview with Evar, I was able to interview Josh Robertson, a vice president of content management at Indaba Music, to further understand the implementation of badges on the site. For Robertson, badges provide alternative gratification to monetary or tangible goods:

Badges are a way to add this element of gaming, of this element of recognition in a way that you don't have to reward people just for winning based on quality. There's other ways to reward people. For instance, there're badges that we give out based on participation. If you enter a certain number of opportunities, you become a certain opportunity level. It could be ten or fifty or a hundred, so that encourages participation and [there is] this gaming element that isn't based purely on skill and talent. … I think that badges and gaming elements are things that are inherent to human psychology. The reason why you do them is just for that simple fact that people like to be rewarded for their activities even if it's something as small as a digital badge for participating in ten things. It's still worthwhile.

Robertson commented that the Indaba community complained about the disappearance of the badges when the site took them away during a time of transition and change. The Indaba blog announced this transition on July 29, 2010, and stated that the site would not be down for more than twelve hours. From the perspective of the Indaba founders and executives, badges are one way in which to encourage the participation of musicians without giving out other material rewards. Although the system could be considered a gamified experience, a large number of musicians have nevertheless been mostly unaware of the badges' existence or have expressed little desire to acquire them. To this end, a disconnect may exist between the intention of the developers and the widespread awareness among the community members.

Halavais (2012) notes that "given that badges are intended to be a visual shortcut, it is important that they remain stable and recognizable" (370). To this end, I inquired whether musicians regularly notice the badges on user profiles and if the badges hold any significance for them. Although not every musician's profile has earned a badge, what is the overall level of recognition tied to the badges? Seventy people (29.9 percent) stated that the badges were somewhat important, and sixty-six people (27.6 percent) described their reaction to the badges as negative. Only forty people (17.8 percent) responded positively to the badges, and fifty people (20.7 percent) replied that they had not noticed the badges. The remaining twenty respondents (8.3 percent) indicated that they didn't care about the badges.

When asked if badges can realistically serve as a way to help others recognize musicians' skill sets or achievements (and to ultimately function as a musician's digital resume), eighty respondents (34.2 percent) replied positively; the second largest response group, seventy-two responses (30.8 percent), was ambivalent. The "I don't know" category received fifty-one responses (21.8 percent), and the negative category received thirty-six (15.4 percent). These numbers indicate that musicians are, in general, uncertain whether the badges can be professionally helpful.

The open responses provide some valuable insights into how musicians perceive badges as an alternative credentialing method. Many replies focused on demystifying the value of the badges; overall, the musicians did not assign the badges any specific significance or meaning. Rather, the badges were understood as inanimate objects of questionable benefit: "Badges seem very immature and unprofessional. People should be reading through your skills, not looking for dumb little pictures" (Indaba survey). Another musician stated that badges are "just a symbol. It really speaks nothing about the person. It's just a

ribbon. Great minds and talents are not made with achievements or awards. They are won with compassion and wisdom."
The survey respondent continued: "The badges mean nothing
because they are nothing more than tiny icons representing how
long you've been working on Indaba." However, this person did
not seem to understand that other badges are earned by being a
contest winner or finalist.

The issue of the badges' questionable value was picked up
by another survey participant, who stated that "the badges are
awarded by someone and music is a thing which cannot be
judged by an individual. I do not know how the person was
judged, so I cannot make a decision about their level of talent." Another musician in the survey also gave the critique that
badges cannot be a representation of one's talent:

Well, because I don't think all the people that have badges have them
because of their "talent" and more so their popularity which has nothing to do with who they are as a musician. People who have badges
should have them because they are great talented Musician[s], Artist[s],
or Producers. People can buy views to make Indaba think they are a good
artist which sucks!

The dismissive attitude toward badges resurfaced in other survey
responses: "some of which have no merit, i.e., popular vote winners." These responses reveal that much of the issue pertains to a
lack of understanding about the badges, although there is clearly
some understanding of how they could work as an alternative
credentialing method:

I am not very knowledgeable on the subject of profile badges on any
website or social network, but I imagine that the effectiveness of such
badges would depend on their criteria for attainment. If they are intended to indicate a particular status, affiliation or achievement, then I
suppose that's a good way to give information to profile visitors up-front

without requiring them to search through various other elements of a user's profile. (Indaba survey)

Another reason why musicians on Indaba Music were not supportive of the idea of badges had to do with their skepticism about whether the website can serve as a place to network and showcase digital e-portfolios.

Indaba music simply isn't a professional enough forum for such achievement recognition, not to mention the voting system is flawed to a "Hot or Not" algorithm for leaderboard recognition, thus disqualifying great submissions for honorable mentions. The website is merely a tool to get your name out, grow as a musician, and have fun collaborating or speaking with other musicians. It is not a site that reflects the skill level or quality of an artist's work. The badges mean nothing because they are nothing more than tiny icons representing how long you've been working on Indaba. (Indaba survey)

Echoing other musicians' skepticism about the objectivity of the musical criteria, another musician also noted that "badges mean that some[one] out there thinks you're talented; while that's nice and all, no one else is gonna take their word for it, people have to listen to your material [and] decide for themselves if they like your material" (Indaba survey). Other musicians conceived of badges in a quantifiable way and did not understand that there were other badges besides the badges one can gain by entering contests. "Number of entry badges doesn't convey the quality of one's work, only the number of contests one has entered. I suppose it shows dedication, but not necessarily talent. Popular vote winners are a joke, because the voting system is a joke" (Indaba survey).

In light of Halavais's (2012) point that "to create a badge system that is mindful of that history, it is important that the intended function of the badges be understood" (370), there was a lack of understanding or awareness about how badges are generally earned on Indaba Music. One survey participant stated: "Anyone who pays can have a badge; skills and accomplishments have no bearing." It seems as though this member was referring to badges one earns through a paid membership with Indaba Music. To this end, it was clear that there was no accurate understanding of the value that the badges themselves held; in comparison, getting recognition was more important than acquiring the badge. A similar misunderstanding was expressed by another musician who claimed that badges "can give a guideline that someone has given the time and effort in their projects, but I wouldn't say it holds a tangible meaning" (Indaba survey).

Overall, the open-ended survey revealed that hardly anyone had deep thoughts or opinions about the badges. In fact, many idealistic responses related to the very nature of music: "The badges are awarded by someone, and music is a thing which cannot be judged by an individual. I do not know how the person was judged, so I cannot make a decision about their level of talent" (Indaba survey). Another respondent noted:

A badge for winning contests doesn't give any information on what level of competition there was or even what genre the competition was. If the badges do anything, they just indicate that that particular user happened to have a quality mix that fits with what those particular judges were looking for. (Indaba survey)

Echoing the concern over prejudice toward badges mentioned by Davidson, the musicians displayed dismissive attitude towards the badge system. With this in mind, I asked them to think about whether or not the badges can effectively represent their talents and accomplishments. One musician replied: "I feel as though 'badges' can help if they effectively denote something of significant importance." It was clear that despite

Indaba's intention, badges were not highly valued by the users. The musicians' perceptions of the value of badges were important because, to some extent, the community of Indaba Music cocreates their significance. One reply stated that badges have brought the musician more collaboration and work: "Having a badge has brought a lot more serious inquiries about music and helped me collaborate with many different artists from around the world." Another survey participant stated: "Badges helped in getting exposure. My profile isn't viewed all that often due to my relative inactivity, but after the badge was added, I received many hits in the few days following. I feel the badge gives you a bit of legitimacy if nothing else."

Badges create incentives to compete. They also bring a game element to the site to increase participation. Another musician noted that badges can bring "more fans. And people feel if you are getting badges, they want to know why, so they click on your music" (Indaba survey). Clicking thus operates as a seal of approval by the community. Finally, there was one extremely optimistic opinion about the badges. For this musician, badges can be a positive reflection of one's level of achievement and skill:

I try to do my best in everything I do—the badge is simply feedback that tells me I did something right. I think others who have tried and failed can use the badges as guidelines/examples to help them become better contributors. Receiving a badge means a lot to me because there is soooo much talent on indabamusic.com. (Indaba survey)

Clearly this musician understands that the badges relate to a value statement, one embedded in the overall community's talents and skill sets. Despite this individual endorsement, the greater issues deal with the ability to communicate beyond the Indaba Music communities.

Motivations for Musicians

The musicians' perceptions of badges help us understand varying motivation levels and values inside the community. In the
context of education, motivation operates as one of the positive
merits of implementing badges (Barker 2013; Abramovich et al.
2013). However, as Barker also pointed out, "[Overemphasizing]
the badges as an external reward for learning [could reduce] the
learners' intrinsic motivation to learn" (253). In contrast to this
view, in the case of interest-driven creative communities such
as Indaba Music, this apprehension was not borne out. The survey indicated the following motivations to enter the contests:
148 (66.6 percent) stated that their primary and strongest motivation to enter a contest or opportunity was the potential for
professional connections, and the next highest motivation was
prize money (99 participants, or 44.6 percent). Feedback was a
motivator for 95 people (42.8 percent). Earning a badge was the
least popular motivation with 21 responses (9.5 percent), and
9.9 percent of the respondents answered "None of the above."

For musicians, badges function as a mere visual recognition
of participation in a specific contest. As Deci (1972) noted, "A
person is intrinsically motivated if he performs an activity for no
apparent reward except for the activity itself" (113). Many musicians echoed this point. A similar account of motivation in terms
of creativity was echoed by Krueger and Krueger (2007): "Intrinsic motivation is a major source of creativity" (6). However, one
should not automatically assume that creative producers are
completely uninterested in external rewards or recognition. In
his seminal work *Creativity*, Csikszentmihalyi (2009) insightfully
notes that "one should not expect that the strong intrinsic motivation of creative individuals needs to exclude an interest in

fame and fortune" (426). This is an important point to remember when considering badges and honors. Although creative producers like musicians are motivated intrinsically, one cannot claim that all artists are motivated only by intrinsic pleasure, nor do artists who desire external means of recognition necessarily lack intrinsic motivations. Reputation building is a central part of artistry for artists, according to Becker (1982), and to this extent, desiring recognition can be natural.

Can Digital Badges Represent Honor and Reputation?

The value of badges as alternative credentialing lies in the idea that the quantity of badges one has acquired matters less than what the badges represent. There are many types of unique badges, but how can one make others understand the selective nature and meaning of the badges while also arguing that they hold universal significance? If badges are to represent an alternative means to evaluate musicians' reputations, badges must have a symbolic appeal, or else they will be ineffective in breaking down the valorization of the number games.

One of the benefits of earning badges can be their potential to represent multiple subjectivities in terms of musical values. Rather than emphasizing how many badges one has earned, the process of earning badges could potentially be a useful assessment system that focuses on celebrating a wide range of tastes, provided that what the badges represent becomes valued. This would be helpful to musicians who are opposed to popularity as a gauge of success but value the endorsements from the competition judges. In this sense, badges could indicate both unique selectivity, such as a "judges' pick," and universal values, as in having popular appeal. Badges can represent both individuality and collectivity without creating an unnecessary hierarchy between the two. Nevertheless badges still face inherent problems and challenges owing to music's ability to communicate in and of itself.

According to Holt (2007), "Musical sound is a symbolic form of representation" (5). The notion of music's symbolic meaning was also echoed by several survey participants: "Music is not a thing" (Indaba survey). Many musicians did not wish for their music to be judged as a commodity; as one musician noted, it is a "vibration" (Indaba survey). What seemed to trouble many musicians was the objectification of music's value. Given music's ability to transcend feelings and self-expression, what other symbols lay behind music's value?

Previously we established that the badges' assets are that (1) they can potentially interrupt a hierarchical conception of evaluation that privileges quantity, and (2) they can function as an endorsement of multiple subjectivities. How do we understand the badges' function as visual communicators when music can also be communicated symbolically? Music does not need additional enhancement or assistance to convey its quality or value, so what place and meaning do visual symbols such as badges have in the musical realm? Echoing several musicians' earlier responses, one may challenge the notion of badges by raising the point that listening to music is itself an act of judgment. Most importantly, this issue is more complicated when considering the rhetoric of "one-hit wonders," which translates to many as someone who has had one hit single but has not had success thereafter in his or her career. In other words, previous success does not guarantee a future outcome, and thus musicians' process of gaining credentials does not result from one positive outcome but will continue over time. While gaining one badge may earn some level of credentialing, a musician will continue to prove himself or herself under constantly evolving musical standards, which means that one badge would not suffice as a symbol of honor; this means it would need more than one badge. Therefore, the criteria for musical evaluation may once again focus on valorizing quantity over quality of badges.

Although Indaba Music has given values to the badges, they did not translate clearly to the users in the form of shared meaning. However, this does not mean that Indaba Music has failed in implementing the badges. What needs to be understood is that much of this meaning must be created collectively within the site. Yet these collective values are also shaped by how they are being translated to the outside world, as well as how the outside community assigns values to them. This is similar to how brand value operates, echoing Arvidsson's (2006) observation that "brand value is built through the appropriation of solidarity and affect generated in a plurality of different circumstances" (89). To some extent, for the badges' values to be understood collectively, they must have the ability to communicate throughout multiple communities. As Rughiniş and Matei (2013) maintain: "If badges are to support public reputations, holders must make them visible and 'translate' them for external observers" (88). While this can happen via the agency of the users, the greater, significant impact will need to come from the actual industry, which must impose meaning before the members within the communities collectively enable it. Then an increase in the significance of the badges will follow naturally. To this end, one cannot ignore the cultural aspects unique to the industries, communities, and educational fields that desire to implement badges as an assessment system. Not only should one ascertain what is valued within a particular culture, but one should also question the prevailing mode of ideology, as well as the common cultural practices that uniquely shape that industry or field. To this end, the research into badges should not just remain at the level of a reductionist inquiry on pragmatics, such as asking, "Does the badge mean anything to the users?" or "Has it truly inspired musicians to gain more recognition?" An ethnographic understanding of the relevant communities is integral to understanding the badges' uses and effects. Additionally, this effort should not just focus on the uniqueness of newly emerging communities in digital spaces; the inquiry must dovetail with several commonly shared views associated with achieving success and recognition in the popular music industry.

To this extent, Frith's (1988) discussion of how musicians achieve success in the industry before the digital era is important to consider. The first method was a pyramid method whereby working hard and building a résumé were rewarded with success. The second method was the talent pool model, where nothing guaranteed success except the erratic nature of the music industry's reliance on chance. Although the success earned from the talent pool model did not guarantee continued success, honor, and prestige, it was still a viable method of earning success. In my previous research, I argued that these two models are still taking place in digital environments; on the one hand, hard work via earning popularity is rewarded, and on the other, being somewhere at the right time and place works (Suhr 2012). ascertain

As noted in the talent pool model, if one believes in the existence of luck, success in the popular music industry does not always come as a result of hard work or talent. This is true if we consider the musicians who are actively working in the music industry and maintaining a certain level of success but have not been trained in an accredited university or music school. Unlike the educational fields or the informal learning communities in which a degree or certificate testifies to one's credentials to a certain level, in the popular music industry, the opposite scenario exists. For some musicians, a lack of experience or credit ironically creates a favorable effect, as many talent shows reveal (e.g., Susan Boyle).

To this extent, how do musicians whose learning often exists outside institutional or formal contexts find their own niches of credentialing?[1] According to Bourdieu (1984), an autodidact or self-learner will always be considered illegitimate owing to a lack of cultural capital:

> The old-style autodidact was fundamentally defined by a reverence for culture which was induced by abrupt and early exclusion, and which led to an exalted, misplaced piety, inevitably perceived by the possessors of legitimate culture as a sort of grotesque homage. (84)

Bourdieu would clearly argue that self-taught musicians are excluded from all possibilities to gain credentials. However, for popular musicians, learning often takes place in informal learning environments or in tandem with formal education. Green's (2007) in-depth study about how popular musicians learn highlights the need to bridge two different learning contexts, the formal and the informal.

In digital environments, the credentialing opportunities for self-taught musicians are ubiquitous. For instance, Ito (2010) analyzes the rewards connected to Japanese noncommercial fan-made music videos. The standards and norms are not aligned with those of the mainstream industries, and the fan cultural producers desire recognition and values that are uniquely shaped within their specific community. Clearly, in a subculture community that practices open access, amateur creativity is valued for its own sake without the teleological aim of recognition or profit from the mainstream industry. But what happens when the process of credentialing occurs in an exclusive context?

In Seiter's (2008) comparison of classical piano skill acquisition with young people's development of digital media skills, she notes how limited financial resources influence the acquisition of cultural capital. With exposure to both instruments and learning opportunities, a pianist can eventually gain recognition through a prestigious music teacher's social network. Much of this process is exclusive in nature, since access is permitted only to those who can afford expensive training with a renowned teacher. In line with Seiter's point about the parochial entryway for musicians seeking to excel and gain recognition in the classical music field, McCormick (2009) points out that, in classical music, "the music competition is a professionalizing institution in the field of cultural production that controls the distribution of symbolic capital (i.e., prestige)" (6).

In reflecting on these conditions and limited access,[2] we can make an analogy with Indaba Music. If Indaba Music is mainly seeking to increase its number of paid annual memberships, for whom are these badges a useful indicator? Do they advance the musicians' careers, or do they solely benefit Indaba Music by motivating musicians to engage in its competitions? How should the communities that issue badges impose their power in terms of credentialing if they are profiting from users who are competing and seeking to increase their reputations? Should musicians have to be paying members? Should they be able to compete without payment? Where does the boundary lie between efforts to create a legitimate method of credentialing musicians and the agendas of profit-driven corporations? Should the sites that issue badges go through a particular review process to ensure that they are legitimate? Much of this issue is complicated by the drawing of symbolic boundaries (Lamont and Fournier 1992).

Lamont and Fournier discuss the importance of understanding how symbolic boundaries are created and the social consequences thereof. Although an elaboration of the different views of symbolic boundaries by sociologists is beyond the scope of this report, the question of inclusion and exclusion is pertinent to the current discussion about access to opportunities.

In other words, to what extent is open access important to universal credentialing? How do each community's differing sets of norms and cultures create unique distinctions? For Indaba Music, the users' primary goal is to gain mainstream access; thus the recognition conveyed by the digital badges within the community did not seem to affect the musicians' motivations, since this required further bridging their symbolic value within the greater community context (i.e., the entire music industry).

Additionally, a potential concern may arise if badges have too much explicit power and value. Previously, the number of friends on Myspace mattered so greatly that services to mechanically aid in this process increased (Suhr 2010). Similarly, YouTube views have been so important that several record labels have faced accusations that they were trying to manipulate the number of views for their artists' videos (Gayle 2012). These few examples alone show how acquiring badges could potentially result in the same type of politics and manipulation, especially in light of Mantis Evar's comment about people wanting to "buy" badges. This is an especially interesting discrepancy considering the survey and interview outcomes, since many of the participants did not find much meaning in acquiring badges.

One of the interviewees also mentioned that he had received an e-mail from a separate service company, offering to help raise the number of listeners, a statistic that matters in the early stages of the contests. Although the musician did not subscribe to this service, he had honestly been tempted to give it a try to see if it could improve his performance during a particular contest. To this extent, having a greater unifying significance of badges may result in misleading representations of reputation owing to the potential abuse of the system.

Conclusion

Much like the evaluation crisis in education, music communities face a similar watershed. On one hand, this is due to the inherently ineffable and inexplicable nature of music. But on the other hand, it has to do with the issue of precarious credentialing processes within the popular music industry. Although gradual shifts have occurred through the rise of social media, the prevailing mode of ideology, centered on concrete, quantitative values as opposed to arbitrary evidence of success, may generate resistance to a reform of the system.

If competitions and chart systems are an integral part of the music industry's core activities, would a symbolic understanding of music's values, in its inherent opposition to any credentialing system, be feasible? Will the music industry be receptive to a more complex way to evaluate artists, when it has previously and successfully relied on the penchants of audiences, even to the extent of tracing the evolving tastes in music?[3] While badges seem to function as enhanced indicators of musicians' talent, at least in terms of what is being valorized in digital environments today, the real question is how to bridge the divide with the music industry. Furthermore, where should we place symbolic capital? Does it exist within the music industry itself or outside its borders? This is the most important question that has not yet been settled. If the acquisition of symbolic capital lies outside the commercial market, who determines Bourdieu's so-called rules of art? Although it may seem as if digital environments have blurred the lines between the commercial music industry and grassroots or underground musicians, digital environments have actually heightened the shaping of these boundaries through the systemization of the grassroots or underground music communities. Yet it is important to keep in mind that the potential to gain connections within the mainstream music industry motivated musicians to join and participate in the contests.

In other words, musicians seem to be embracing the online presence of traditional gatekeepers, since many musicians still believe that persisting toward traditionally conceived dreams of success, achievable through determination, luck, and hard work, is important. One of the individuals with whom I spoke in person continually emphasized that "he is not naive" about the end goal of the process. Despite being aware of the arbitrariness of the competition process, many musicians seem to believe that they must pursue as many opportunities as possible, since no universal entryway or system to gain approval and credentialing exists.

Finally, we must realize that addressing these questions cannot just be the sole effort of scholars or musicians. Educators, technology companies, scholars, critics, and musicians should all be involved in the deeper discussion and debate. Closing down or dismissing prematurely the potential of badges as a credentialing method would be a mistake. Thus in this chapter, I have critically explored badges' potential as an alternative means of assessment. Furthermore, I have analyzed the challenges that badge designers, educators, and the music industry, as well as musicians themselves, must confront as we think about the future trajectory of the assessment system.

5   Digital Badges in Music Communities and Digital Evaluations

In this report, I explore digital badges as an alternative evaluation practice by focusing on two music communities that have adopted digital badges. Two primary concerns can be compared in both communities. The first pertains to using digital badges as an alternative evaluation method. How does Spotify's evaluation game compare to Indaba Music's activities, since both communities use digital badges as a means to create gamified environments where learning can take place?

Spotify and Indaba Music use two different methods of evaluation. Spotify's evaluating game concentrates solely on the hit potential of songs. Therefore music evaluation on Spotify is grounded in the combination of understanding participants' personal musical tastes, ability to discern hit potential, and user enjoyment. The evaluation process on Spotify is conditioned by the logic of the market and conceived to produce a certain outcome related to recognizing what makes a hit in today's music industry.

On Indaba Music, the evaluation process is more complex. Unlike Spotify's focus on a sharp binary measure to evaluate music, such as likes versus dislikes, hit or not, on Indaba Music, earning a badge requires a lengthier process (not a matter of a few seconds or minutes, as on Spotify). Upon agreeing to enter a contest, a musician's tracks are judged by peers through a voting method. In addition to voting (open to members of the community, as well as nonmembers), an algorithm on Indaba Music generates a Hot Track status. Although the subject of algorithms and Hot Tracks will be explored at length elsewhere, the Indaba Music algorithm picks up quantitative comments made by contestants. To be successful, musicians need to both promote themselves and gain peer endorsements. What is rewarded in the community is thus active participation. Finally, a rotating panel of judges selects the winning tracks. When musicians accumulate numerous votes and are selected as finalists or winners, they acquire different types of badges representing various achievements.

Second, what roles do digital badges play for evaluators and those being evaluated? The evaluators of music feel no strong motivation to earn digital badges. At best, digital badges might express one's personal musical taste, thus revealing an aspect of personal identity. However, many of the badges were generic or connoted a certain sociological understanding of tastes, such as "hit maker" (referring to liking commercial music) versus "hipster" badges (implying esoteric tastes not shared by many people). Other badges, such as "hit predictor," also reflected how one's tastes were aligned with mainstream hit potential. To this end, to consider digital badges as an extension of one's musical tastes is rather far-fetched. Furthermore, evaluators in general did not place much meaning or value in acquiring digital badges, thus revealing an apathy toward what the digital badges represent.

As for musicians who are evaluated, similar to Hit or Not game players, they do not seem to be driven to acquire digital badges. For the most part, musicians rarely need any additional motivation, as they are usually innately driven to create, share, and compete. Besides intrinsic goals, musicians' other motivations relate to potentially gaining connections in the music industry. To this end, digital badges have little significance overall. Unless digital badges hold collective value inside and outside of Indaba Music, it seems unlikely that badges will function as symbols of prestige or reputation. In the meantime, it is important not to lose sight of the other means to evaluate music. Digital badges are just one out of many emerging evaluations in today's digital environments. Over time, new evaluative criteria and norms will emerge and shape musical standards, and researchers will be confronted with new ways to conceptualize them. To this end, I offer an open-ended definition of digital evaluation to reflect on possible future research directions.

What Is Digital Evaluation?

1. Digital evaluation takes into account "transient environments," thereby recognizing the potential for such mechanisms to vanish or to adopt a different or new form. In fact, the digital evaluation paradigm seeks, in part, to trace such mechanisms; to some extent, it creates a history of how the arts and creativity have been critiqued and accessed in digital environments, exploring both dominant and discursive modes of evaluative practices as they relate to creativity and the arts.

2. Digital evaluation locates itself between empirical research and the humanities; while much of the study of digital environments comes from an empirical point of view, occurring within the qualitative study of interviews, textual analysis, content analysis, and ethnography, the overarching framework addresses broader concerns invoked within the discipline of digital humanities.

3. Digital evaluation has a symbiotic relationship with learning, but much of the definition of learning in relation to digital evaluation is open to broad interpretations. Self-taught learning is a discrete category in artistic environments. Therefore, what does it mean to teach creativity and to learn about creativity? What do cultural producers, the industry, and participators of evaluation learn from these related processes? Because many of the commenting and rating activities are openly disseminated and given directly to the artists, the artists' or cultural producers' self-reflexivity is recognized as an important learning experience. Furthermore, critics and the media industry can also learn about what appeals to mass tastes.

4. While digital evaluation has a temporal dimension, whereby the emphasis is on discerning the evolution and mutation of the evaluative mechanisms in digital environments, the issue does not merely boil down to providing an analysis of hype-driven activities. Although these phenomena offer a snapshot of history, digital evaluations of the arts and creativity explore timeless and ontological questions beyond the descriptive analysis of alternative evaluation activities. In other words, these evaluations unpack enduring questions such as the following: What is at stake at the height of the commenting, rating, ranking culture? How do we wrestle with the dichotomy of subjectivity versus objectivity, amateur criticism versus expert critique? What types of practices closely align themselves with this dichotomy?

5. While the nature of the analysis invokes abstraction, not every context of evaluation of creativity explores the subjectivity of tastes. Some analysis explored in this report pertains to a more practical understanding within market research of consumers' tastes, while other practices explored here relate to the complexity of shaping artistic and creative content. For example, one

of the representative aspects of evaluation activities today is the rampancy of ranking. Although ranking implies having an order, does this order shape itself in digital environments, or are there calculated efforts in which this order is pronounced?

6. Digital evaluation recognizes that the order of artistic tastes and creativity can be shaped in a variety of ways: overtly or subtly imposed, or collectively created in hegemonic tensions. This variety echoes Carroll's (1987) analysis of Foucault's argument: "The ultimate foundation of order is not in itself or any metaprinciple, but in the instability of disorder inherent in all order" (56). Much of the order given to artistic merits is often pronounced and planned by the architectural foundation of the social media services themselves; while some instances may show that order or hierarchy is formed through bottom-up efforts by consumers, order can be top-down in nature depending on the criteria of assessment inherent in each context. Sometimes order is shaped through synergistic efforts between user participation and site rules and criteria, which are adaptable according to the nature of participation and vice versa. Overall, digital evaluation seeks to explain how each artistic and creative community has evolved and negotiated the meaning-making process in terms of (1) setting, (2) negotiating and collaborating, or (3) resisting the assessment criteria, process, and practices.

Conclusion

This chapter seeks to raise preliminary inquiries in the discussion of digital evaluations as a valuable potential framework from which to study the emerging phenomenon of rating, ranking, critiquing, and evaluating in digital environments. On the one hand, these questions and explorations are important ones from a practical point of view—the careers of creative producers are sometimes at stake, and it is important to question how legitimate and fair the evaluations are in their impact on artists' and cultural producers' reputations and credentialing. On the other hand, these casual practices have further theoretical and pedagogical implications in their configuration and how they affect the standards of music and the arts. As different types of cultural intermediaries emerge, we are confronted with the question of whether the democratic participation by everyday consumers and Internet users should result in their having a stake in evaluating artistic practices. In this vein, it is my hope that this report can ignite a new debate about some of the challenges and pressing questions at the epicenter of the judgment and evaluation culture.

Notes

Introduction

1. Digital environments here include those related to online environments and digital devices.

4   Underpinning Digital Badges as a Symbol of Honor

1. In discussing the popular music industry, I am referring, in general, to the U.S. popular music industry. In other countries, such as South Korea, popular music (K-pop) artists that are under evaluation for formal contracts must go through a rigorous, extended, formal training process under the major record labels.

2. In problematizing this idea, I am by no means asserting that musicians are avoiding these contests because they fear potential exploitation; as I argued elsewhere, as well as in this report, such concerns are not prominent for musicians.

3. This trend needs to be noted with the roles that Myspace played initially in promoting new artists within the industry, as well as for emerging artists in an independent and unsigned context.

References

Abramovich, S., C. Schunn, and R. M. Higashi. 2013. Are badges useful in education? It depends upon the type of badge and expertise of learner. *Educational Technology Research and Development* 61:217–232.

Adorno, T. W. 1945. A social critique of radio music. *Kenyon Review* 7 (2): 208–217.

Adorno, T. W. 1998. On popular music. In *Cultural Theory and Popular Culture: A Reader*, ed. J. Storey, 197–209. New York: Prentice Hall.

Adorno, T. W. 1978. On the fetish character in music and the regression of listening. In *The Essential Frankfurt School Reader*, ed. A. Arato and E. Gebhardt, 270–299. New York: Bloomsbury Press.

Adorno, T., and Horkheimer, M. 2002. The culture industry: Enlightenment as mass deception. In *Dialectic of Enlightenment: Philosophical Fragments*, ed. G. S. Noerr, 94–137. New York: Routledge. (Original work published 1944.)

Ahlkvist, J. A. 2011. What makes rock music "prog"? Fan evaluation and the struggle to define progressive rock. *Popular Music and Society* 34 (5): 639–660.

Amabile, T. M. 1996. *Creativity in Context: Update to "The Social Psychology of Creativity."* Boulder: Westview Press.

Anderson, T. 2014. *Popular Music in a Digital Economy: Problems and Practices for an Emerging Service Industry*. New York: Routledge.

Arvidsson, A. 2006. *Brands: Meaning and Value in Media Culture*. New York: Routledge.

Ash, K. 2012. "Digital Badges" would represent students' skill acquisition: Initiatives seek to give students permanent online records for developing specific skills. *Education Week Digital Direction*. http://www.edweek.org/dd/articles/2012/06/13/03badges.h05.html?tkn=ORSF1.

Austin, J. R. 1990. Competition: Is music education the loser? *Music Educators Journal* 76 (6): 21–25.

Barker, B. 2013. Digital badges in informal learning environments. Paper presented at ICIW 2013, the Eighth International Conference on Internet and Web Applications and Services.

Becker, H. 1982. *Art Worlds*. Berkeley: University of California Press.

Belk, R. W. 2007. *Handbook of Qualitative Research Methods in Marketing*. Northampton: Edward Elgar.

Bhagwan, V., T. Grandison, and D. Gruhl. 2009. Sound index: Charts for the people, by the people. *Communications of the ACM* 52 (9): 64–70.

Blom, D., and K. Poole. 2004. Peer assessment of tertiary music performance: Opportunities for understanding performance assessment and performing through experience and self-reflection. *British Journal of Music Education* 21 (1): 111–125.

Bourdieu, P. 1984. *Distinction: A Social Critique of the Judgement of Taste*. Cambridge, MA: Harvard University Press.

Breen, M. 1990. Billboard goes into technological overdrive to make radio hits. *Popular Music* 9 (3): 369–370.

Brennan, M. 2006. The rough guide to critics: Musicians discuss the role of the music press. *Popular Music* 25 (2): 221.

Brown, H. 2012. Valuing independence: Esteem value and its role in the independent music scene. *Popular Music and Society* 35 (4): 519–539.

Burnard, P. 2007. Reframing creativity and technology: Promoting pedagogic change in music education. *Journal of Music, Technology, and Education* 1 (1): 37–55.

Carroll, D. 1987. *Paraesthetics: Foucault, Lyotard, Derrida*. New York: Taylor & Francis.

Carroll, N. 2000. Art and ethical criticism: An overview of recent directions of research. *Ethics* 110 (2): 350–387.

Chamorro-Premuzic, T., and A. Furnham. 2007. Personality and music: Can traits explain how people use music in everyday life? *British Journal of Psychology* 98 (2): 175–185.

Chong, E. K. M. 2011. Blogging transforming music learning and teaching: Reflections of a teacher-researcher. *Journal of Music, Technology, and Education* 3 (2–3): 2–3.

Cook, N. 2000. *Music: A Very Short Introduction*. New York: Oxford University Press.

Csikszentmihalyi, M. 2009. *Creativity: Flow and the Psychology of Discovery*. New York: HarperCollins.

Dale, P. 2009. It was easy, it was cheap, so what? Reconsidering the DIY principle of punk and indie music. *Popular Music History* 3 (2): 171–193.

Deci, E. L. 1972. Intrinsic motivation, extrinsic reinforcement, and inequity. *Journal of Personality and Social Psychology* 22 (1): 113–120.

De Saussure, F. 2011. *Course in General Linguistics*. New York: Columbia University Press.

Desztich, R., and S. McClung. 2007. Indie to an extent? Why music gets added to college radio playlists. *Journal of Radio Studies* 14 (2): 196–211.

Domínguez, A., J. Saenz-de-Navarrete, L. De-Marcos, L. Fernández-Sanz, C. Pagés, and J.-J. Martínez-Herráiz. 2013. Gamifying learning experiences: Practical implications and outcomes. *Computers and Education* 63:380–392.

Dunn, K. 2012. "If it ain't cheap, it ain't punk": Walter Benjamin's progressive cultural production and DIY punk record labels. *Journal of Popular Music Studies* 24 (2): 217–237.

Finnas, L. 1987. Do young people misjudge each other's musical taste? *Psychology of Music* 15 (2): 152–166.

Frith, S. 1988. *Facing the Music: A Pantheon Guide to Popular Culture*. New York: Pantheon Books.

Frith, S. 1996. *Performing Rites: On the Value of Popular Music*. Cambridge, MA: Harvard University Press.

Frith, S. 2000. Music industry research: Where now? Where next? Notes from Britain. *Popular Music* 19 (3): 387–393.

Frith, S. 2002. Fragments of a sociology of rock criticism. In *Pop Music and the Press*, ed. S. Jones, 235–246. Philadelphia: Temple University Press.

Galuszka, P. 2012. Netlabels and democratization of the recording industry. *First Monday* 17 (7). http://firstmonday.org/ojs/index.php/fm/article/view/3770/3278.

Gaut, B. 1998. The ethical criticism of art. In *Aesthetics and Ethics: Essays at the Intersection*, ed. J. Levinson, 182–203. New York: Cambridge University Press.

Gayle, D. 2012. YouTube cancels billions of music industry video views after finding they were fake or "dead." *MailOnline*. http://www.dailymail.co.uk/sciencetech/article-2254181/YouTube-wipes-billions-video-views-finding-faked-music-industry.html.

Glejser, H., and B. Heyndels. 2001. Efficiency and inefficiency in the ranking in competitions: The case of the Queen Elisabeth Music Contest. *Journal of Cultural Economics* 25 (2): 109–129.

Goligoski, E. 2012. Motivating the learner: Mozilla's Open Badges program. *Access to Knowledge: A Course Journal* 4 (1): 1–8.

Gracyk, T. 2007. *Listening to Popular Music; or, How I Learned to Stop Worrying and Love Led Zeppelin*. Ann Arbor: University of Michigan Press.

Grammy 365. http://www.grammy365.com.

Green, L. 2007. *How Popular Musicians Learn: A Way Ahead for Music Education*. Burlington, VT: Ashgate.

Haan, M. A., S. G. Dijkstra, and P. T. Dijkstra. 2005. Expert judgment versus public opinion: Evidence from the Eurovision song contest. *Journal of Cultural Economics* 29 (1): 59–78.

Halavais, A. M. C. 2012. A genealogy of badges. *Information Communication and Society* 15 (3): 354–373.

Hamari, J., and V. Eranti. 2011. Framework for designing and evaluating game achievements. In *Proceedings of DiGRA 2011: Think Design Play*. Hilversum, Netherland, September 14–17.

Hardt, M., and A. Negri. 2000. *Empire*. Cambridge, MA: Harvard University Press.

Hargreaves, D. J., D. Miell, and R. A. MacDonald. 2002. What are musical identities, and why are they important? In *Musical Identities*, ed. D. J. Hargreaves, D. Miell, and R. A. MacDonald, 1–20. Oxford: Oxford University Press.

Hearn, A. 2010. Structuring feeling: Web 2.0, online ranking and rating, and the digital "reputation" economy. *ephemera: theory and politics in organization* 10 (3–4): 421–438.

Hennion, A. 2001. Music lovers: Taste as performance. *Theory, Culture, and Society* 18 (5): 1–22.

Hennion, A. 2007. Those things that hold us together: Taste and sociology. *Cultural Sociology* 1 (1): 97–114.

Hesmondhalgh, D. 1999. Indie: The institutional politics and aesthetics of a popular music genre. *Cultural Studies* 13 (1): 34–61.

Hogan, B. 2010. The presentation of self in the age of social media: Distinguishing performances and exhibitions online. *Bulletin of Science, Technology, and Society* 30 (6): 377–386.

Holbrook, M., and R. M. Schindler. 1989. Some exploratory findings on the development of musical tastes. *Journal of Consumer Research* 16 (1): 119–124.

Holt, Fabian. 2007. *Genre in Popular Music*. Chicago: University of Chicago Press.

Hunter, D. 1999. Developing peer-learning programmes in music: Group presentations and peer assessment. *British Journal of Music Education* 16 (1): 51–63.

Indaba survey. 2012. 255 survey entries. Retrieved from Surveymonkey .com (currently the survey is closed).

IFPI. 2013. *IFPI Digital Music Report 2013: Engine of a Digital World.* http://www.ifpi.org/downloads/dmr2013-full-report_english.pdf.

Ito, M. 2010. The rewards of non-commercial production: Distinctions and status in the anime music video scene. *First Monday* 15 (3). http://firstmonday.org/ojs/index.php/fm/article/view/2968/2528.

Ito, M., H. A. Horst, M. Bittanti, B. Herr-Stephenson, P. G. Lange, C. J. Pascoe, and L. Robinson. 2009. *Living and Learning with New Media: Summary of Findings from the Digital Youth Project.* Cambridge, MA: MIT Press.

Jaret, C. 1982. Hits or just heartaches: Characteristics of successful and unsuccessful country music songs. *Popular Music and Society* 8 (2): 113–124.

Jenkins, H. 2006. *Convergence Culture: Where Old and New Media Collide.* New York: NYU Press.

Jenkins, H. 2012. How to earn your skeptic "badge." *Confessions of an Aca-Fan: The Official Weblog of Henry Jenkins.* March 5. http://henryjenkins.org/2012/03/how_to_earn_your_skeptic_badge.html.

Jones, C., and A. King. 2009. Peer learning in the music studio. *Journal of Music, Technology, and Education* 2 (1): 55–70.

Kant, I. 1952. *The Critique of Judgement.* Trans. J. C. Meredith. London: Oxford University Press.

Kapp, K. M. 2012. *The Gamification of Learning and Instruction: Game-Based Methods and Strategies for Training and Education.* San Francisco: Pfeiffer.

Keen, A. 2008. *The Cult of the Amateur: How Blogs, MySpace, YouTube, and the Rest of Today's User-Generated Media Are Destroying Our Economy, Our Culture, and Our Values.* New York: Doubleday.

Kozbelt, A. 2008. One-hit wonders in classical music: Evidence and (partial) explanations for an early career peak. *Creativity Research Journal* 20 (2): 179–195.

Krueger, J., and J. Krueger. 2007. *Culture and Economy: A Distinct Relationship*. Munich: GRIN.

Langer, S. K. 1966. The cultural importance of the arts. *Journal of Aesthetic Education* 1 (1): 5–12.

Lamont, M., and M. Fournier. 1992. *Cultivating Differences: Symbolic Boundaries and the Making of Inequality*. Chicago: University of Chicago Press.

Lebler, D. 2008. Popular music pedagogy: Peer learning in practice. *Music Education Research* 10 (2): 193–213.

Lee, J. J., and J. Hammer. 2011. Gamification in education: What, how, why bother? *Academic Exchange Quarterly* 15 (2): 146.

Lee, S. 1995. Re-examining the concept of the "independent" record company: The case of Was Trax! records. *Popular Music* 14 (1): 13–31.

Levinson, J. 1996. *The Pleasures of Aesthetics: Philosophical Essays*. Cambridge: Cambridge University Press.

Lieb, K. 2013. *Gender, Branding, and the Modern Music Industry: The Social Construction of Female Popular Music Stars*. New York: Routledge.

Lingel, J., and M. Naaman. 2011. You should have been there, man: Live music, DIY content, and online communities. *New Media and Society* 14 (2): 332–349.

Liu, H. 2008. Social network profiles as taste performances. *Journal of Computer-Mediated Communication* 13 (1): 252–275.

Lomas, N. 2013. Basno raises $1M for its digital badges platform that aims to monetize boasting. *Tech Crunch*. http://techcrunch.com/2013/07/02/basno-1m-badges/.

Marti, S., and H. Garcia-Molina. 2006. Taxonomy of trust: Categorizing P2P reputation systems. *Computer Networks* 50 (4): 472–484.

McCormick, L. 2009. Higher, faster, louder: Representations of the international music competition. *Cultural Sociology* 3 (1): 5–30.

McDaniel, R., R. Lindgren, and J. Friskics. 2012. Using badges for shaping interactions in online learning environments. Paper presented at the Professional Communication Conference (IPCC), 2012 IEEE International.

Miller, R. E. 1994. A dysfunctional culture: Competition in music. *Music Educators Journal* 81 (3): 29–33.

Mōri, Y. 2009. J-pop: From the ideology of creativity to DIY music culture. *Inter-Asia Cultural Studies* 10 (4): 474–488.

Muntean, C. I. 2011. Raising engagement in e-learning through gamification. Paper presented at the 6th International Conference on Virtual Learning, ICVL.

Negus, K. 1995. Where the mystical meets the market: Creativity and commerce in the production of popular music. *Sociological Review* 43 (2): 316–341.

Negus, K. 1998. Cultural production and the corporation: Musical genres and the strategic management of creativity in the U.S. recording industry. *Media Culture and Society* 20 (3): 359–379.

Negus, K. 1999. *Music Genres and Corporate Cultures*. New York: Routledge.

Negus, K. 2002. The work of cultural intermediaries and the enduring distance between production and consumption. *Cultural Studies* 16 (4): 501–515.

Newman, J. 2011. The Zune is dead? Then why these new apps from Microsoft? *Tech Hive.* http://www.techhive.com/article/237212/the_zune_is_dead_then_why_these_new_apps_from_microsoft_.html.

Nicholson, S. 2012. A user-centered theoretical framework for meaningful gamification. Paper presented at Games Learning Society 2012, Madison, WI.

Papaioannou, T. G., and G. D. Stamoulis. 2006. Reputation-based policies that provide the right incentives in peer-to-peer environments. *Computer Networks* 50 (4): 563–578.

Papastergiou, M. 2009. Digital game-based learning in high school computer science education: Impact on educational effectiveness and student motivation. *Computers and Education* 52 (1): 1–12.

Parker, M. 1991. Reading the charts: Making sense with the hit parade. *Popular Music* 10 (2): 205–217.

Parkins, C. 2008. Indaba Music. Creativecommons.org. https://creative commons.org/weblog/entry/8099.

Payne, E. 1967. Musical taste and personality. *British Journal of Psychology* 58 (1–2): 133–138.

Raymer, R. 2011. Gamification: Using game mechanics to enhance elearning. *eLearn Magazine* 9 (3).

Rentfrow, P. J., and S. D. Gosling. 2006. Message in a ballad: The role of music preferences in interpersonal perception. *Psychological Science* 17 (3): 236–242.

Rentfrow, P. J., J. A. McDonald, and J. A. Oldmeadow. 2009. You are what you listen to: Young people's stereotypes about music fans. *Group Processes and Intergroup Relations* 12 (3): 329–344.

Rudolph, T., and J. Frankel. 2009. *YouTube in Music Education*. New York: Hal Leonard.

Rughiniș, R. 2013. Badge architectures in engineering education: Blueprints and challenges. In *Fifth International Conference on Computer Supported Education (CSEDU)*.

Rughiniș, R., and S. Matei. 2013. Digital badges: Signposts and claims of achievement. In *HCI International 2013: Posters' Extended Abstracts*, 84–88. New York: Springer.

Russell, P. 1997. Musical tastes and society. In *Social Psychology of Music*, ed. D. J. Hargreaves, 141–158. New York: Oxford University.

Ruthmann, S. A. 2007. Strategies for supporting music learning through online collaborative technologies In *Music Education with Digital Technology*, ed. J. Finney and P. Burnard, 230–225. New York: Continuum.

Sargent, C. 2009. Local musicians building global audiences: Social capital and the distribution of user-created content on- and off-line. *Information Communication and Society* 12 (4): 469–487.

Scott, M. 2012. Cultural entrepreneurs, cultural entrepreneurship: Music producers mobilising and converting Bourdieu's alternative capitals. *Poetics* 40 (3): 237–255.

Segrave, K. 1994. *Payola in the Music Industry: A History, 1880–1991*. Jefferson: McFarland.

Seiter, B., and E. Seiter. 2012. *The Creative Artist's Legal Guide: Copyright, Trademark, and Contracts in Film and Digital Media Production*. New Haven, CT: Yale University Press.

Seiter, E. 2008. Practicing at home: Computers, pianos, and cultural capital. In *Digital Youth, Innovation, and the Unexpected*, ed. T. McPerson, 27–52. The John D. and Catherine T. MacArthur Foundation Reports on Digital Media and Learning. Cambridge, MA: MIT Press.

Selfhout, M. H. W., S. J. T. Branje, T. F. M. ter Bogt, and W. H. J. Meeus. 2009. The role of music preferences in early adolescents' friendship formation and stability. *Journal of Adolescence* 32 (1): 95–107.

Shumway, D. 2008. Questions of pleasure and value. In *The Aesthetics of Cultural Studies*, ed. M. Berube, 103–116. Malden: Blackwell.

Sisario, B. 2013. What's Billboard's No. 1? Now Youtube has a say. *The New York Times*. February 20, 2013. http://www.nytimes.com/2013/02/21/arts/music/billboard-makes-youtube-part-of-hot-100-formula.html?_r=0.

Smith, H. 1988. Badges, buttons, T-shirts, and bumperstickers: The semiotics of some recursive systems. *Journal of Popular Culture* 21 (4): 141–149.

Strachan, R. 2007. Micro-independent record labels in the UK: Discourse, DIY cultural production, and the music industry. *European Journal of Cultural Studies* 10 (2): 245–265.

Stratton, J. 1982. Between two worlds: Art and commercialism in the record industry. *Sociological Review* 30 (2): 267–285.

Stratton, J. 1983. Capitalism and romantic ideology in the record business. *Popular Music* 3:143–156.

Suhr, H. C. 2008. The role of participatory media in aesthetic taste formation: How do amateurs critique musical performances and videos on YouTube.com? *International Journal of Technology, Knowledge, and Society* 4 (2): 215–222.

Suhr, H. C. 2009. Underpinning the paradoxes in the artistic fields of MySpace: The problematization of values and popularity in convergence culture. *New Media and Society* 11 (1–2): 178–198.

Suhr, H. C. 2010. Understanding the emergence of social protocols on MySpace: Impact and its ramifications. *Comunicar: Scientific Journal of Media Education* 17 (34): 45–53.

Suhr, H. C. 2012. *Social Media and Music: The Digital Field of Cultural Production*. New York: Peter Lang.

Terranova, T. 2004. *Network Culture: Politics for the Information Age*. Ann Arbor: Pluto Press.

Thelwall, M., P. Sud, and F. Vis. 2012. Commenting on YouTube videos: From Guatemalan rock to El Big Bang. *Journal of the American Society for Information Science and Technology* 63 (3): 616–629.

Tschmuck, P. 2012. *Creativity and Innovation in the Music Industry*. New York: Springer.

Waits, J. C. 2008. Does indie mean independence? Freedom and restraint in a late 1990s U.S. college radio community. *Radio Journal: International Studies in Broadcast and Audio Media* 5 (2–3): 2–3.

Waldron, J. L., and K. K. Veblen. 2008. The medium is the message: Cyberspace, community, and music learning in the Irish traditional music virtual community. *Journal of Music, Technology, and Education* 1 (2–3): 2–3.

Warf, B., and J. Grimes. 1997. Counterhegemonic discourses and the internet. *Geographical Review* 87 (2): 259–274.

Wikstrom, P. 2010. *The Music Industry: Music in the Cloud*. Cambridge: Polity Press.

Young, J. R. 2012. "Badges" earned online pose challenge to traditional college diplomas. *Education Digest: Essential Readings Condensed for Quick Review* 78 (2): 48–52.

Zwaan, K., T. F. ter Bogt, and Q. Raaijmakers. 2009. So you want to be a rock 'n' roll star? Career success of pop musicians in the Netherlands. *Poetics* 37 (3): 250–266.

The John D. and Catherine T. MacArthur Foundation Reports on Digital Media and Learning

Digital Youth with Disabilities by Meryl Alper

Peer Participation and Software: What Mozilla Has to Teach Government by David R. Booth

The Future of Thinking: Learning Institutions in a Digital Age by Cathy N. Davidson and David Theo Goldberg with the assistance of Zoë Marie Jones

Kids and Credibility: An Empirical Examination of Youth, Digital Media Use, and Information Credibility by Andrew J. Flanagin and Miriam Metzger with Ethan Hartsell, Alex Markov, Ryan Medders, Rebekah Pure, and Elisia Choi

New Digital Media and Learning as an Emerging Area and "Worked Examples" as One Way Forward by James Paul Gee

Digital Media and Technology in Afterschool Programs, Libraries, and Museums by Becky Herr-Stephenson, Diana Rhoten, Dan Perkel, and Christo Sims with contributions from Anne Balsamo, Maura Klosterman, and Susana Smith Bautista

Young People, Ethics, and the New Digital Media: A Synthesis from the GoodPlay Project by Carrie James with Katie Davis, Andrea Flores, John M. Francis, Lindsay Pettingill, Margaret Rundle, and Howard Gardner

Confronting the Challenges of Participatory Culture: Media Education for the 21st Century by Henry Jenkins (P.I.) with Ravi Purushotma, Margaret Weigel, Katie Clinton, and Alice J. Robison

The Civic Potential of Video Games by Joseph Kahne, Ellen Middaugh, and Chris Evans

For more information, see http://mitpress.mit.edu/books/series/john-d-and-catherine-t-macarthur-foundation-reports-digital-media-and-learning.